Division of Surgery

Division
of Surgery

Donna McFarlane

women's
P R E S S

CANADIAN CATALOGUING IN PUBLICATION DATA
McFarlane, Donna, 1958–
    Division of surgery

ISBN 0-88961-193-9
1. McFarlane, Donna, 1958–   . 2. Inflammatory bowel diseases
— Patients — Fiction. I. Title.

PS8575.F37D5 1994   C813'.54   C94-930515-4
PR9199.3.M34D5   1994

copyright © 1994 Donna McFarlane

Editing: P.K. Murphy
Copy editing: Lynda Nancoo
Cover design: Sherree Clark and Rooth MacMillan
Author photo: © 1994 Edward Gajdel

This book was produced by the collective effort of Women's Press.
Women's Press gratefully acknowledges the financial support of
the Canada Council and the Ontario Arts Council.

Printed and bound in Canada
1 2 3 4 5 1998 1997 1996 1995 1994

Acknowledgements

I am grateful for the assistance of The Canada Council Explorations Program and the Ontario Arts Council.

Division of Surgery began as a series of half-hour broadcasts on *Life Rattle*, a story show on CKLN FM radio (in Toronto). Thanks to *Life Rattle* co-hosts Arnie Achtman for his constant and invaluable help in the writing of this book, and Guy Allen for his advice and encouragement. Without their generous assistance this book would not exist.

Thanks also to my friends Julia Scalzo, Laurel Goodings, Pia Jensen, George Robinson, Michele Metraux, Ron Bloore and the McFarlane family.

For Arnie

PATHOLOGY REPORT
Toronto Memorial Hospital

Patient's Name:	D.O.B.
Carr, Mrs. Robin	14/02/58

Physician/Surgeon	Date Received	13 Nov. 1984
Dr. Coleman	Date Reported	23 Nov. 1984

COLON

Operation: Subtotal colectomy and ileostomy.

Preop: Ulcerative Colitis

The specimen consists of 80 cm. of bowel. At one end the appendix, the ileocecal valve, and caecum are identified. The distal end has no distinguishing features. The distal 35 cm. of bowel is markedly abnormal and there is a sharp demarcation line between this and the proximal bowel which appears quite unremarkable in that its wall is thin and flexible. The amount of serosal fat is not in excess and the mucosal surface is thrown into small folds and it is generally smooth. The more distal segment, however, is abnormal in that there is a slight increase in the amount of serosal fat, the wall is thin and nonflexible, the mucosal surface is raised with rough irregular polypoid lesions, and there is a haemorrhagic discolouration to the mucosal surface. These changes are more marked distally and gradually decrease over the proximal 15 cm. of the 35 cm. of affected bowel. The appendix measures 10 cm. in length and 5 mm. in diameter and its surface is unremarkable.

Comment:

The colon shows extensive ulceration with acute and chronic inflammatory changes of mucosa. The terminal ileum is free of disease. There is no evidence of epithelial atypia or malignancy. Five sampled lymph nodes are unremarkable in appearance.

DW/my

tissue code	Dr. D.W. Chambers

In Public

I sat in the corner of Mr. Greenjeans, in the corner of the Eaton Centre, my back to the wall, as far from the other customers as the hostess allowed. I sipped tea. Six weeks earlier the Prophet had cut out my diseased bowel leaving me with an ileostomy, a plastic bag full of warm shit hanging from my side. I hated the bag, even though it had saved my life. I feared what its odour could reveal about me.

I sniffed the Earl Gray tea before I sipped it. I scanned the restaurant. After two months in the hospital, I expected to see white coats, surgical greens and tube-bound patients hunched against pain. Instead I saw black pants and white shirts covered by green butcher's aprons as five young waiters rushed from the kitchen carrying orders. Speakers blared wordless high-pitched Christmas carols. I noted the location of the washrooms.

On the table before me lay application forms: Pension Income Security Program, Unemployment Insurance, and York University's Staff Association Long-term Disability Program. Women alone in restaurants have to do something; the forms disguised my waiting for my next appointment with my next doctor. I saw my waiter, a white-skinned, straight-backed, blond boy, hesitate at the coffee station and poach a drag from a cigarette. He looked up. I dropped my gaze to avoid his.

Half an hour before, I'd had my first appointment as a post-surgical out-patient with Dr. Coleman. He had cauterized the weeping opening of an eight-inch tunnel that ran from my inactive rectum to the skin at the left of my abdomen. He called this hole, ringed with tiny black knots of suture thread, a fistula. I'd kept a medical dictionary by my hospital bed so I could look up their words. Now I carried it with me to these appointments like a tourist.

Mucus leaked steadily through their fistula and my rectum; Dr.Coleman suggested cauterization and dressing, though he said the success varied.

I sipped tea then touched the gauze dressing under my baggy, dark wool trousers. It still seemed dry. My eyes lowered to my belly and watched my hand make its peculiar journey to the right to feel my ileostomy bag. I hated the gesture, yet I made it constantly, unsure and inexperienced with the bag's security and capacity. I remembered my father touching his abdomen with the same anxiety.

My father had an ostomy too. It had not halted the advance of his disease or lessened his pain, although it did extend his life. My father appreciated the reprieve. I questioned it. I had often wished him dead, so the pain would pass. Surgeons had rushed through an emergency surgery, formed his ostomy poorly. I knew from my father the humiliation of an ostomy that leaked. I inhaled, smelt nothing, grateful for the skill of the Prophet's hands.

I looked around the restaurant, searching for quarry for my name game. In the abattoir, when all I could count on was my mind, I had learned to distract myself with the name game. The hospital became the abattoir. Dr.

Coleman, the surgeon, became the Prophet. Dr. Zucker-mann, the psychiatrist, was the Wizard of Oz.

Across the restaurant I watched a woman in a high-necked maroon dress sitting across from a man in a standard blue business suit. They appeared WASP, like my parents might have looked thirty years ago. The woman's legs twisted tightly together, lightly stroked each other, the curve of one foot nestled into the arch of the other. The heels of her navy blue pumps looked chewed. She raised her hand to her forehead, shielding her eyes and squinting under green neon. Mole. Yes, I'll call her Mole. Let me see, who else?

My gaze caught the wall mirror. Below garlands of plastic holly I saw a thin, fragile woman, a waif. I flinched. Dark circles shadowed eyes hollowed by exhaustion. Vertical strain lines creased between my brows. My hands trembled slightly as I lifted my fingers to my mouth. In two months, I had lost my large intestine, thirty pounds and most of my muscle. Who could love such an emaciated, pale, brittle woman?

I recalled the supple, compact poise of my husband's body. When we first met in university, I had watched Joseph train on rings every evening, making whirling circles with muscle stretched, ankles held securely together, his concentration as he soared rotating in space above the mat, his controlled sudden thud as he hit the mat and his arms raised to a wide V above his head. I remembered the broad smile Joseph gave when he saw me in the stands. Now he coached gymnastics for children. How could I keep up?

My eyes focused again in the mirror. Two women stared back at me from behind a mound of open textbooks. One pushed her oval black-wire glasses up on her pointy white nose, pulled her thin lips taut over her teeth and mouthed to the other. The second kept her pen balanced above her sheets of foolscap but glanced at my reflection and shook her head slowly from side to side to side. I ran my hands from my brow, over my head to the nape of my neck and dropped my gaze to the table in front of me. Despite the close-to-the-skull cut of my hair, strands covered the table. I was losing my hair too. Tapering off steroids does that sometimes. They think I'm ugly now, they should have seen me on I.V. steroids.

In the ward's mirror, over several days, I had watched steroids inflate my face to a puffy white moon. My knees ballooned to the size of basketballs, too stiff for me to squat to the floor. Joseph and I called the humped collection of fluid in my shoulders a buffalo back. A delicate growth of hair over my jaw, black like my older brother's beard but not coarse, drew no comment from Joseph. I worried I'd never look like myself again. My usually black hair had faded to dull red from malnutrition. How could both images, fat then skeletal, be mine within weeks? "Fascinating", Joseph remarked to a nurse, while visiting me. More fascinating if it's someone else, I thought.

A curt, mini-skirted hostess flicked her lacquered curls as she directed a pretty couple to the table beside mine. I shifted my hips away from the man as he manoeuvred between the tables to the bench beside me. The woman sat across from him, struggling with her winter coat. I glanced at her hand and saw no wedding ring. I twisted my band, too loose on my withered ring-finger, and inspected the man. He exuded well-studied, artistic warmth. He wore earth tones. Golden brown and gray hair fell in waves around his collar. The skin on his nose was peeling. His cheeks glowed from a suntan. His dark eyes solicited and held her attention easily. I christened him Prince Charming.

I burrowed through my purse and eavesdropped.

The Prince moved with the self-confidence of a performer, a magnificent flirt. I tried to ignore him but he even smelled good, not antiseptic, like the doctors, but with a sensual, groomed masculinity. The velvety green-gray fragrance of talc hovered in the air beside me.

I inhaled deeply but smelled my own muffled stink: either ooze under my gauze dressing or flesh newly-burnt by the Prophet's cauterization. Wondering if anyone else noticed, I retrieved the bottle of perfume Joseph had given me from the bottom of my purse, sprayed one wrist with the scent of roses and rubbed it against the other.

My father kept sheets of fabric softener in his pockets to disguise the smell of his ostomy and had my mother buy all brown underwear for him. Brown so she, his wife of 32 years, could not see his ostomy through his briefs. Brown, so she would be less aware of his stains when she did the laundry. I switched my underwear to black, even though Joseph now left the room when I undressed, even though I did the laundry.

I asked my mother, "Will I smell like Dad?"

"No, you won't let yourself", she said. "Your father is going to die. He has bigger things to worry about than smell."

After my father's surgery, two years before mine, he offered my mother a divorce while the family sat around the living room watching a basketball game on tv. I stared at my father, but he kept his eyes fixed on my mother. My parents never spoke intimately in the presence of my brothers or me, so I got up to leave the room.

"I'm not the same man you married."

I moved toward the door.

"Of course not." My mother glanced at me then laughed, "You're 32 years older and we have three children."

"I'm not whole." My father touched his ostomy, his mouth open as he stared at my mother.

"Whole?" I pivoted to speak to my father. "You're still the same. It comes out there or it comes out here. What's the difference? No one cares." I left the room and the rest of the conversation to my parents.

But Joseph cared. He no longer showered with me. I worried I repulsed him. If I changed my ileostomy, a fifteen-minute procedure, he left the apartment for three hours. He said he went to the gym to exercise. He begged me to have cosmetic surgery, skin grafts to cover my scars. I told him surgery hurt and I planned to avoid unnecessary pain. We hadn't touched since I came home four weeks ago.

"I'm afraid to hurt you." Joseph squirmed my hand away from his shoulder.

"I'll tell you if it hurts."

"I don't think you're being responsible."

In his sleep but with his eyes open, Joseph lifted the covers and asked me if I bled. When I told him I was all right, he demanded I raise my nightgown to prove it. In the morning he recalled nothing.

The packets of sterile bandages, the micro-pore tape, the skin prep, the rubber gloves, the extra ostomy bag clip and the bottle of ostomy deodorant, he removed from our medicine cabinet whenever friends came to visit.

"Don't tell anyone," he said.

"But they know I had surgery. And I'm going to have two more."

"Yes, but they don't know what an ostomy is and soon it won't matter."

He told me my father and I had intestinal disease because my mother didn't keep her kitchen clean enough. He said our marriage would get better when my housekeeping did. Joseph said people became ill from carelessness.

A click sounded as the Christmas carols started another cycle, the third since I arrived in the restaurant.

I unzipped the back compartment in my purse and dug past my emergency kit — new flange, ostomy bag, scissors, stomahesive paste, gauze compresses and panties — to the slender brown-plastic vial that held the last of my steroids and pain medication. A chart written in my mother's hand on a blue index card showed the correct time and reduced amount of steroid. Half a pill at three o'clock. I stroked the dose off the list. Three days and two doses remained.

Beside me the Prince leaned forward and spoke softly. I strained to hear him, as I popped the lid off the pill container, pulled out the cotton, tipped one pill into my palm, then placed it on the plate before me. I took aim with a bread knife at the tiny indentation in the pill's middle and pressed down. The pill shattered, leaving half on the plate. The other half, in fragments, flecked him. He brushed off the lapel of his moss-green corduroy jacket without a glance toward me.

"I wonder," the Prince said, "Will your kiss be tentative?"

So sincere, so sensitive, so sweet. He just has to be a prick.

I dipped my hand inside my purse, fingered the long cylinder of silver nitrate applicators. The Prophet prescribed burning the fistula on my side with these six-inch match-like sticks until it healed, or until my next surgery in June. The first surgery had lasted five hours; the next promised six. The same mid-line incision would open my abdomen. The Prophet had slit through my abdomen like sliced layers of onion.

Did he really expect me to burn myself? It's only the top layer, but the odour. How can I do it so Joseph won't notice?

Platters of bleeding burgers with fries arrived for Prince Charming and his princess. She dumped red muck over her fries.

I looked away. Eating revolted me. Food had caused such pain in my now-missing bowel that I still harboured a deep distrust of eating by mouth. For five of the eight weeks in the abattoir I had eaten nothing, drank nothing, had no medication by mouth. I was fed through T.P.N., a tube implanted into an artery under my collarbone. It seemed cleaner, neater, a more efficient method. It's hard to tell the poison from the cure, I thought as I took the half Prednisone pill with tea.

The waiter circled again. My menu lay open under the forms. I didn't want food but I knew the chair I sat in was only rented. I pulled out the menu and surveyed it with one hand cradling my ileostomy. There must be something here I can eat. Salads, too much fibre. Meat, too bloody. Tacos, too hard. Chicken wings, too spicy. Pasta, too much.

In my mind I saw an image of a fleshy garden hose, red and swollen with disease, heaped in a garbage can. What do they do with removed organs anyway? I shuddered. I could still see the Prophet at the foot of my hospital bed, surrounded by his students, as engrossed in him as disciples in their master. Seven heads towering over me and seven pairs of eyes peering down upon me, their only interest my bowel, my disease and what I could tell about them.

"Robin, turn on your side please," the Prophet said, as he pulled the curtain around my bed. The interns, all men, in white lab-coats like the Prophet's, gathered round to consider my anus while the Prophet explained the next surgery.

"The patient is repositioned in the lithotomy Trendelenburg position. Construction of the J-shaped pouch and mucosal proctectomy are performed simultaneously. The J-shaped pouch is constructed by folding the 15 to 20 centimetre limb to the left side of the patient. The pouch is constructed preferably using a two-layer, hand sewn entero-enteric anastomosis of catgut and Vicryl. Alternatively, G.I.A. and T.A.-55 staplers can be used. Although staplers are quicker, they have several disadvantages: closing the enterotomies with the T.A.-55 stapler foreshortens the pouch slightly; the longitudinal stretching of the pouch down the anus against these transversally closed enterotomies has produced four leaks at the staple line in our series. We strongly suggest that the anastomosis be performed by a hand-sewn suture technique. Since using a hand-sewn technique exclusively, we have not encountered leaks in 22 patients."

Having concluded his lesson, the Prophet and his disciples left the room.

To quell terror and humiliation, I asked lots of questions. I didn't always understand the answers, nor did they always answer me, but I needed to let them know

I had a mind as well as a body. Daily, for two months, they had probed and pressed on my swollen belly, stuck their fingers into my diseased and bloody rectum, shoved needles into my bruised arm, then left me to clean myself up and pull together what little dignity remained.

The Prophet stood five-foot six-inches. The nurses joked he worked from a ladder during surgery. I saw him alone just twice, but he saved my life. He saw my tears before surgery, my agony — despite the morphine-induced haze — after surgery. Common sights for him; empty beds in the intestinal surgery unit were scarce. I remembered trying to memorize his hands, wanting to touch them as I was wheeled past him flat on my back into the cold green operating room. For our most intimate contact I had been asleep, anaesthetized. He had been inside me with a knife, and I had consented to it.

"Your eyes deceive you," cut in the Prince's voice from the next table.

This princess is a dolt if she buys this crock.

The waiter appeared. I grinned at him. My smile went unreturned. Oh go to hell, I thought, and smiled on.

"Anything else?" he demanded.

"Do you have any dessert that isn't gigantic?"

"Cheesecake: plain or chocolate." He pointed to the lower corner of the plastic menu.

"Plain and another Earl Gray please," I said. Cheesecake's soft. It won't hurt me.

I pictured my father in his brown tweed sports-jacket sitting across the table from me. He wore one of his favourite ties, a red and green tartan, purchased from the Neighbourhood Services for a nickel. For special occasions we were allowed to choose between The Marco Polo or Caesar's Pizza. It was my eleventh birthday. Dad had sat stroking the cowlick on his crown, studying the menu. I sat on my hands. Dad ordered.

The waiter said, "Drinks? Coffee? Dessert?"

Dad shook his head. "No, but I'd like to hold on to the menu."

I blushed.

After the waiter left Dad said, "Instant coffee costs less than five cents a cup." He tapped the menu. "It's not worth seventy-five cents." He closed the menu. "Your mother has birthday cake at home."

I checked my wallet. Cheesecake might cost as much as five and tea, another one. I had ten dollars and subway tokens.

The cheesecake arrived. I used the fork like a scalpel, making patterns in its soft white flesh. The line ran from the space between the last rib, around the belly button to my pubic hair. I traced that line again and again in the cheesecake. I am alive because of this line, I chanted silently. I am alive because of this line. The Prophet has the hands of a priest. The Wizard has wonderful straight, white teeth. The Wizard of Oz makes me lie down on that damned couch and talk. I don't have anything to say. I hate lying down for him. I laid down for another doctor and look what happened.

Toward 4 p.m., the restaurant filled, mostly with people in their mid-twenties like me, but in groups or couples, and they all ate.

Everyone else in here has a colon, I bet.

My ileostomy gurgled as new waste slid down the inside of the plastic bag. No one heard. No one glanced up. No smell.

I won't have this for long, I vowed. Six months, a year max. I'm going to have a pelvic pouch. Then no one, not even Joseph, will know that I don't have a bowel. Just a scar on the outside, no bag. I'm going to be normal.

That is how I came to call Dr.Coleman, the Prophet. He had invented and perfected a surgical technique to make a bag, a sort of reservoir, out of a section of the remaining small intestine, and place it inside the body just above the rectum, so it could be controlled by the sphincter muscle and emptied through the anus.

A miracle. I just have to wait for the time to pass and these things will disappear. The Prophet said so.

The cheesecake tasted plain indeed, but it took thirty minutes to eat and adequately covered my eavesdropping. Prince Charming's hand extended and brushed a lock of hair from the woman's face. I ached to intercept that touch, a tender touch, not a clinical one.

"Your hair's lovely," he said gently.

I wonder what the Prince would do if he got this woman home and started to undress her only to discover she had an ileostomy? Ha! I wonder how sincere he'd be then? Sincerely horrified or sincerely sorry?

I looked down and waited as the second hand hesitated at each mark on my watch's face. Quarter-to-four, time to see my psychiatrist. Amazing what a little dose of mortality could spur me to do. Fear of death is how I finally got to hug the Wizard of Oz. Who would have thought I could hug my psychiatrist in my pyjamas without guilt?

I folded the Pension Income Security Program form, the Unemployment Insurance form, the York University Staff Association Long Term Disability form into thirds, wrestled them into their respective business-sized envelopes and shoved them in my purse. Taking a last glimpse at the couple beside me, I fingered the warm metal of the teapot. Maybe I can spill some tea on this prince-of-a-guy as I get up to leave.

I did.

Mark Coleman, M.D., F.R.C.S.(C)
Toronto Memorial Hospital
Evens Building, 9-539
101 Academy Street
Toronto, Ontario

in association with:
L.Bander, MD, FRCS (C)
W.Johnson, MD, FRCS (C)
N.R.Pryce, MD, FRCS (C)
U.Arbus, MD, FRCS (C)
B.R.Smith, MD, FRCS (C)
L.E.Goldstein, MD, FRCS (C)
R.S.MacDonald, MD, FRCS (C)

November 4th, 1985.

Dr. Jeff Axon
130 Newcastle Avenue
Toronto, Ontario

Dear Jeff,

RE: CARR, Robin

I saw Robin in the office today and she is coming along very well, despite her initial slow recovery. The drainage tube was fully removed and the area in the perianal region is now completely healed. There has been no further build up of pus and certainly no further drainage.

On examination the anal anastomosis is somewhat tight due to the scarring from the local surgical repair but I could dilate this easily with my finger.

I think Robin will achieve a good result from her pelvic pouch. I will now wait an additional 6 months before closing her loop ileostomy and re-establishing gastrointestinal continuity.

I am not sure if I mentioned in my last note to you that she has had considerable difficulties with her husband and is now separated from him. This has been an extra upset for her.

I have made arrangements to see her again in the office in one month.

Best regards,

Yours Sincerely,

Mark Coleman, MD, FRCS(C)

MC/jb

In the Alley

"He caught my nipples, pinched them hard and jerked me forward. 'Come here,' he said and I thought I had no choice. 'I'm going to fuck you,' he said next. He pressed my mouth, jammed in his tongue. He pulled me down to the floor. 'Get on your knees.' And he took me from behind. That's how I think of him."

Lucy glanced at me. She turned onto Claxton Boulevard, pulled her Toyota to the curb in front of my apartment building, pushed the stick shift to park, and turned off the headlights.

"So why do you see him?" Lucy stared hard at me.

"I feel trapped. It's been eighteen months since I left Joseph. Then there's this next surgery and being careful all the time. My mother calls me everyday to ask if I'm all right. Even my apartment — so tight and organized — like I'm just waiting to get sick again. I want it to be different. I feel like Goody-Two-Shoes."

"Fat chance," Lucy laughed.

I watched Lucy's cheeks rise and her eyes close as her mouth stretched to a wide smile. I thought about how much I loved her. We had passed the evening drinking single-malt scotch and laughing at the university gossip I'd missed while on long-term disability. We used to work together eight hours a day and still phone each other on weekends. Lucy worked as the administrator of

York University's theatre department. For five years I'd worked as her assistant. She came to my wedding. After my father died she phoned every morning during the week I stayed with my mother. Lucy rented a van and helped me load my possessions, when I left my husband. Hers was the first pregnancy I had watched on a daily basis. She told me everything that happened to her. Although thirteen years older than I, and five inches shorter, our mannerisms were so alike, that people often mistook us for each other at the university.

I undid my seatbelt and rolled down the car window. "I met him while I was buying my new sewing machine on Spadina." Scotch still burned rich and peaty at the back of my mouth. The night air felt cool on my throat.

"I didn't know you started sewing." Lucy took a cigarette from a pack on the dashboard. She flicked her pewter lighter and the cigarette tip glowed red.

"I'm tired of hearing the sales clerks whisper about anorexia outside the change room when I try to buy clothes. So I decided I'd make my own clothes. Mom used to have bouts of sewing, when my father went away to conferences. She made most of my clothes when I was a child. I'm bored out of my skull not working, so I figure if she could relieve her anxiety productively, so can I."

Lucy nodded. Her cheeks collapsed to hollows as she drew on her cigarette.

"I bought this machine and he was just sitting there. He's a sewing machine mechanic. We talked for a while and he asked me if I'd like a coffee. So we walked up to The Hillcrest, then he said 'I bet your boyfriend is an architect or something. I said, 'I'm separated and my ex is a high school Phys.Ed teacher.' He asked who left who and I just started talking. I couldn't believe myself. I looked at his beautiful green eyes and thought, I wonder if his breath tastes like smoke. I wonder how he makes love. And I felt this sense of freedom. I must have smiled because he asked me what I was thinking. I said 'I've never met anyone like you'. He liked that."

Lucy smiled and held her cigarette out the window.

"Coffee runs into dinner, dinner becomes a walk, a drink, a kiss, sex. It wasn't until after that he told me he had this three-year on-again, off-again relationship with another woman called Nicole."

"Does it make a difference to you?" Lucy caught my eye then glanced out the window.

"Yes and no. But I told him if it's on again, I'm off," I laughed.

"Well if he makes you feel good, that's something." Lucy turned to look at me and pressed her back against the car door.

"I met Serge at Washington University about a year after I left my first husband. I don't think I could have chosen two more different men." Lucy sucked in smoke then let it drift out her nostrils. "I can understand you not wanting to be with someone like Joseph again."

"He's worked twelve years as a sailor. Now he lives in a rooming house off Spadina. Nine other men. Two bathrooms. He lives on the third floor." I reached for Lucy's cigarettes, pulled one from the pack and lightly twisted it between my fingers. "As long as he has enough food and booze and sex, he's happy. I've never known a man so interested in his body's reactions."

Lucy glanced in the rear-view mirror. "What does Zuckermann think?"

"He said, 'It's one thing for me to tell you you're attractive. It's another thing to get laid.'"

"I suppose." Lucy shrugged and tipped her head to one side.

An orange cat sprang onto the still-warm hood of Lucy's car. Lucy jumped. The cat's head looked too large for his body. His left eye swelled closed, blood matting the inside corner. The colour of his fur, like the right side of his face, was handsome.

"He's like that." I pointed my unlit cigarette to the cat peering through the wind-shield at us. "An Alley Cat. A scrapper and a survivor. He's got living all over him. Even if he lives a shorter time he will have lived wilder, freer. I want some of that living." I tapped my finger against the glass. The cat swung its claws. "Hello Richard."

"This is too weird for me, Robin. I know cats, and they don't do that." Lucy stared at the cat on the car hood then stabbed out her cigarette. "You're not going to die." She turned her head, blew smoke out the window, then rolled it closed.

I watched the cat. "If I was going to die I would have during the first or second surgery. This next one is a little procedure. Still I..." I paused and looked at Lucy. I felt a fog of alcohol between my skull and my skin. "I feel how close dying is. I want more life, more experience. I want it quicker."

"Is he inside?"

"No. He doesn't have keys." I looked at Lucy. She gripped the steering wheel.

"You think the cat's rabid or something?"

"It's the 'or something' that I don't want to consider."

Lucy turned the ignition. The cat flattened his ears to his head, hissed and leapt to the pavement.

"Lucy, I never knew you were superstitious."

"Maybe you should think about this." Lucy fastened her seat belt. "I think you're playing with fire, Robin."

"I'll be careful." I kissed Lucy's cheek, got out of the car, paused and glanced around for the orange cat, expecting an attack. Lucy's car tires squealed on the road as she drove away. The shrieks of cats mating behind my building split the night air. I headed for my apartment and wished I hadn't drunk so much.

I fit my key in the glass front entrance, turned it and pulled on the door. The plastic plants in the lobby spun. I leaned against the elevator button.

Don't get sick on the elevator. If you can keep moving you won't get sick. You won't get sick on the stairs.

I pictured the old mahogany staircase in the Alley Cat's boarding house. Two flights, two landings to get to the toilet from his room. On the nights I stayed there I hauled on my floor-length wool dressing-gown despite the intense heat of the top floor and slipped downstairs to the roach-infested toilet, a roll of toilet paper always tucked under my arm. Toilet paper was a luxury I could not count on in the Alley Cat's place.

One morning he pursued me into the bathroom.

"What's all this sanctity of the bathroom? Show me how it works."

"All right." I dropped my black jeans to my ankles and sat on the toilet, the plastic bag directed between my spread legs. "The clip here opens so it can be emptied." I knew he knew that. It opened once during sex and to my astonishment, he hadn't wanted to stop his pounding. "I'm washable, you're washable, so are the sheets," he said. I managed to clip it shut without incident. He passed the test, but I never really trusted him.

I opened the white plastic clip and coaxed the contents of my ileostomy gently down towards the toilet bowl. The stool, the consistency of mashed bananas or lumpy pudding, slid out. I wondered if he'd comment on the difference between it and his own. He sat on the edge of the tub and watched without comment. I proceeded through the ritual: took two small bottles from my purse, rinsed the bag through the bottom opening with water from one bottle, dried the lower edges of the bag with toilet paper so it wouldn't smell, added blue deodorizer from the second bottle to the ileostomy bag and replaced the clip. I flushed and stood.

"Your turn," I said, and hitched my pants.

He sat. I watched and listened and held my breath against the smell, just as he had.

The elevator door opened. I pushed the button for five and leaned against the wall. My stomach seemed to rise with the elevator.

I want a man completely separate from the rest of my life, to desire me just for my body. I want only pleasure from my body. I want lust.

The elevator doors slid open and florescent light stung my eyes as I followed the corridor to my apartment. I turned the key, switched on a lamp in my apartment — one room, a kitchenette, a bathroom — and locked the door. I checked my machine — no messages — opened the fridge and pulled out a bottle of Johnny Walker. Just one more.

I turned on the light in the bathroom, looked around, turned it off. The Alley Cat and I did it once in his bathroom. We never made love; we fucked. I wonder if he makes love with Nicole.

I sat on my Hide-A-Bed and drank.

Joseph and I never fucked. We never made love either. We barely even touched.

I pictured Joseph's mother, Lena. A short woman, her hair piled up in Baroque curls added another five inches to her height. She came to visit me in the abattoir in November 84. Sitting at the foot of my hospital bed, she said, "Perchè accude questo al mio figlio?"

"Lena, you know I don't understand."

She leaned forward in her chair. "I don't think it's fair to Joseph. He goes to work, then he comes here to see you, then he walks that dog of yours, cooks and cleans for himself and goes to sleep, then starts over again. It's too hard on him." I remember studying her black beehive and wondering what to say.

Weighing 105 lbs. I returned home to a filthy apartment. The hospital offered a housekeeper once a week and a visiting-nurse. Joseph declined the housekeeper, saying he didn't want extra traffic in our apartment. He wanted me to clean up. When I told him I couldn't, he refused to help. "I'm tired too," he said. My mother came from Ottawa to put our apartment in order.

"Be patient, he'll come around. I know what it's like for him and it's not easy," my mother advised. "It's hard on him as well, you know."

After two months at home, alone all day, alone most weekends because Joseph drove to St.Catharines to see his family without me, I began to hate his dodges.

One February morning Joseph said, "You need help." He sat at our kitchen table, a photography magazine open in front of him.

We lived on Jane Street, north of Finch in a one-bedroom beige box, one of two hundred and forty other one-bedroom boxes stacked twenty floors high, in a row of three identical buildings. Our families had given us their cast-off furniture. My mother had sewn our curtains. Our fifth floor apartment windows overlooked the gray pavement of our building's parking lot, and a brown brick ice-arena across a street. I kept the curtains drawn whenever possible.

"We need a marriage counsellor." I sat down across from him. "You think it's my fault don't you? You think I owe you because you came to see me in the hospital everyday. Well, you just had to watch. I had to survive it. You had a choice. I didn't."

Joseph smiled with a sad amusement. "And now you think you're better than everyone else because you were sick."

"We're talking about marriage here. And our marriage is boring. We live like brother and sister. I can't stand it."

"I see you looking at men all the time," Joseph inserted a finger between the pages then closed the magazine around it.

"It's not my fault. I need some reassurance. I feel so ugly."

"You're sick. What do you expect?"

"I'm doing my part. I'm seeing a psychiatrist. Maybe it's you that needs the help for a change. You can't even touch me." My voice trembled. Joseph opened his magazine, but kept his eyes on me. "You think we'll go to a marriage counsellor and they'll say it's my fault because I'm sick." Joseph nodded so slightly I wondered if he realized he did it. "It can't all be my fault, and I won't let you blame me. No counsellor in their right mind would say I'm all bad and you're all good. You see a therapist of some sort, anyone, but you have to see them yourself — then I'll see a marriage counsellor with you. I'm not going to do all the work on this marriage, not alone."

Joseph averted his eyes.

"I'll take you seeing a therapist as a sign of active commitment to this marriage. If you don't see one, I'll leave."

In September 1985, I left and moved to this building on Claxton, west of Bathurst, north of St.Clair.

I poured myself another scotch and took off my clothes. I stood and studied myself in the mirror.

The extreme black of my hair, touching the white of my drug-bleached skin, defined my facial and body structure, high, broad cheekbones echoing wide angular hips. Bones protruded everywhere. My withered body had no muscle. No fat softened the frame.

"Where are you?" I said to the mirror.

Before the scars and the ileostomy I'd stood strong and stalwart. At five-foot-seven, 135 lbs. I was what they call a "big girl," muscular, athletic, energetic, independent, arrogant in my health. The baseball and volleyball teams at Riverdale High School in Ottawa nicknamed me "Butch."

My new fragile body was considered more feminine, more attractive to men, more enviable to women, more model-like. From the right angle people said that I looked like a young boy; *Elle* magazine called it the "garçonne look". But now I saw my body as just a container to cart my mind around. I didn't need a man to recognize my mind.

I watched the reflection of my hand stroking my face, from earlobe to jaw, down my neck to my collar bone. I don't want to be alone.

I phoned him, pressing the numbers carefully. The phone rang and rang and rang. I pieced together hockey schedules and concluded he should be home. Imagining the Alley Cat in bed with another woman, I hung up and called again, but the image would not leave, and words came too. His words: he was in bed fucking, slamming, humping, having, screwing, balling, fucking, fucking, fucking Nicole who he insisted on telling me was a hotter, better lay. I pushed his words out of my mind by speaking my own out loud: "The old alley cat's been out finding his pussy all right. I'll just have to wait and see what the old tom has to say — the miserable bastard."

I pulled the bed out of the couch and slept naked on the bare mattress, the bottle of Johnny Walker open on my dresser.

A week later the Alley Cat and I drove north of Algonquin Park to Deux Rivieres on the Ontario-Quebec border. I wanted to go away for a few days. The Prophet had scheduled surgery in Toronto Memorial Hospital for the day after we returned. I had inherited the car from my father. The steering wheel vibrated when the Alley Cat accelerated over 120. His head grazed the car's roof on every bump. The wipers dragged rhythmically against the dull afternoon drizzle. As we travelled up the 400, the gray apartment towers of the Jane-Finch corridor gave way to the papier-maché mountain and rollercoaster tracks of Canada's Wonderland.

North of Huntsville, the radio's reception failing, I

felt bored. I thought the Alley Cat couldn't squirm away from me, so I asked about Nicole.

"Yeah, Nicole was at my place watching the hockey game. It was her birthday and I didn't think she should be alone," he said.

"So why didn't you answer the phone?"

"I knew it was you and I knew you'd be pissed off, so I didn't answer. That's all."

"But —"

"But nothing," he cut me off. "I'll tell you what is going on later. Not now. You're going in for surgery. I'll tell you about it after that. Case closed."

Okay. I'll think about the important stuff. This jerk isn't important. I won't stay with him and he certainly hasn't been faithful to me. I'm just a novelty to him. The real subject is closure. In a few days my ileostomy will be closed. Can it be possible? For two years, I've been in the abattoir every four to six months. They operated. I recovered. I got sick. They operated. Finally the cycle's going to end with my pelvic pouch hooked up to my small intestine. Five surgeries to make my abdomen closed and bagless. Finally, no bag to bang around when I bang. No more lumps of stool on my side. No more bumps under my clothes. No more hand on my abdomen to check if it's full. No more worrying if the person next to me in a public washroom can hear the plastic. Please no more!

Ahead of us an eighteen-wheeler geared down to counter the grade spewing black exhaust above its cab. The highway divided into three lanes. The transport hauled to the right. The Alley Cat pumped the gas pedal until my ten-year old Chevette gained speed, chugged to the centre lane and passed.

"Being a sailor must be wonderful," I said. "All that movement and freedom."

"Freedom?" The Alley Cat snickered, "The ship may be moving but if the captain's on your ass you're cooked."

I leaned my elbow on the window ledge and looked out.

"I sailed to Norway once. Was sea-sick for a week. The Atlantic is much rougher than the Great Lakes. Never got used to the sway." He rocked side to side in his car seat. "I couldn't keep anything down. So when we put into port — I don't remember the name of the place. Me and Bill — Bill really knew how to have a good time. We went out to this fancy restaurant and ate a huge meal. Bill knew a lot about wines. Chablis was his specialty. We had three or four bottles, ten courses, stayed there four hours. Must have dropped a hundred each, left a heavy tip so the waiters were happy.

'We went to a disco after that. We're looking around and there's these Americans — I can tell by their cigarettes — really good-lookers. A couple men, but mostly women. I think, I can get into this. So I'm dancing, having a good time. The woman gets tired so I walk back to the bar and this American guy stops me and says,'Man, you move real good. Where'd you learn how to do that?' We get to talking and I find out he's with an American ballet company that's touring Scandinavia. So I tell him, 'That dance I was doing, I got it from an old Mickey Mouse cartoon. One from the thirties." The Alley Cat grinned. "Blew him away."

"I know that cartoon. I saw it at an animation festival." I said.

"Yeah, I saw you there."

"What?"

"I saw you and your girlfriend at that festival — at The Bloor, right?" He looked at me. "And I thought with a face like that she must be fucking half of Queen Street so I didn't approach you."

I stared through the wind-shield and remembered the Alley Cat standing me up naked in front of one of the many mirrors that surrounded his bed and ordering, "Look."

"What are you talking about?" My hand covered my ileostomy. Standing naked behind me, he tugged my hand away and pressed it to my back. I struggled against him but his clench tightened.

"Look, you're beautiful."

I stared toward his bedroom window. "No, I'm not."

He had held my skull between his large roughened hands, turned my head from the window and forced me to look at my exposed reflection.

"You're beautiful," he persisted.

"No," I yelled, but he held my head still, my gaze fixed to the mirror.

I saw only my scars, my ileostomy. I have to live with it, why should I have to look at it, I thought and stared at his naked body to avoid mine.

His body was heavy, hair ringing his oversized nipples. A high forehead sloped to thick black eyebrows; green eyes peered from beneath. Thinning black hair pulled severely back into a limp ponytail. Often he wore a silver snake earring coiled into the chalky white fold of his ear.

In the mirror, his naked body behind mine, he was handsome in his strength and agility, ugly in his nerve and bad manners — a true alley cat.

I caught my reflection in the Chevette's side mirror. Damned mirrors everywhere.

"Never had a sick lover before," he said.

"Me neither." I closed one eye and looked at him.

He laughed.

The rain cleared by Sundridge. By the turn-off for Highway 94, near Callander, the sun broke through the clouds, a low blush on the horizon over Lake Nipissing.

"So if you're trapped on a ship what do you do?"

"Work mostly." He stroked his black ponytail. "We had bridge tournaments, that sort of thing." He rolled his shoulders forward then back and stretched his neck to either side. "I started sailing at sixteen. Couldn't take it at school any more so I cut out. I was big even then. Lied about my age and got on the *Griffin*, Canadian Steam Ship Lines. We hauled lime." He looked at me. "I still go home every few months to see my mother."

"What was your father?"

"A millionaire." He turned the steering wheel slightly and glanced at me. "And I'm taking you to the fucking family estate for the weekend." He pressed the gas pedal and we passed a station-wagon, its back-end loaded with three kids and a dog.

"And your father?"

"My father was a minister."

He slapped my thigh and hissed with laughter. I looked away. He giggled for what seemed like hours.

At my father's funeral, less than a year before, my younger brother Alan and I had sat side by side listening to music taped for the service. Tears flowed down my cheeks. My father ran the Sunday school and preached every third week in the Ottawa Unitarian church. My mother ran the daycare. Behind the lectern copper enamelled circles picturing scenes of childhood, made by children of the congregation, sat bolted to the wall. I had made six of them when I was ten years old. To either side of the lectern, windows overlooked the Ottawa River. I took many walks with my father along those banks after church.

I quietly snapped my fingers in rhythm and leaned into Alan. He took my hand.

"Do you know this music?" I whispered in his ear.

"I taped it from Dad's favourite Oscar Peterson album." Alan squirmed uncomfortably in his tie and brown suit.

"The words?" I giggled.

Mom glanced over at me, her eyes puffed and red from days of crying.

I sang quietly in Alan's ear, "Missed the Saturday dance. Hear they crowded the floor. It's awfully different without you..."

"Don't get around much any more," Alan sang with me.

We laughed. Mom frowned. Alan sang the second verse to her. Mom, Gordon, Alan and I sat in the front row of the church shaking with laughter while the rest of the congregation watched.

"He would have loved this," Mom said.

The Alley Cat flicked on the car's head lights. "Going into the cabin in the dark will be a real trick."

"And whose fault is it we left so late?" I didn't look at him.

"A night in a motel won't kill you. We can leave early tomorrow morning. Besides game six is tonight."

At Mattawa, as the sun set, we checked into the Valois Motel. Wood veneer panels covered the room's cinder block walls. The bed's headboard shone in orange gold-trimmed plastic. The air stank, heavily scented with Artificial Spring. The Alley Cat snapped on the tv, opened a bottle of gin and flopped back on the bed.

I parted the orange floral-print curtain and watched the electric light from the window cast itself across the Ottawa River to green cliffs on the far shore.

"Wooooo!"

I turned to him. He bobbed toward the tv screen, slapping his knees with excitement, the gin set on the floor between his feet. On the screen ten or twenty players pounded and shoved. The camera panned from cluster to cluster of players beating each other, then tightened its focus on a shirtless Flyer pummelling his gloveless opponent.

"What happened? I thought it hadn't started." I crossed the room and sat on the foot of the bed beside him.

"I've been waiting for this. God-damned Lemieux had it coming. You can't shoot practice shots on the Flyers' net and expect nothing to happen."

The players thrashed for fifteen minutes, the Alley Cat whooping whenever a Canadien bled.

"This is awful. Why don't they stop it? Where are the refs.?"

"It's great. The Flyer's will punish the fucking Habs. The Flyers go for the man all the time, never the puck. They always finish their checks. It's fucking great."

I moved to the top of the bed and propped myself against the headboard to watch the game. The Flyers won 4 to 3. The Canadiens lost the conference. During commercials, the Alley Cat crawled up the bed, rubbed his face and body against me and bit my neck.

After 8 a.m. we drove beside the Ottawa River, on Highway 17 to Deux Rivieres, then turned abruptly onto a logging trail. Using aerial photographs, maps and his childhood memories, we found our way over what only an idiot or a saint would describe as a road. A growth of several feet of brush indicated no vehicles had come this way since autumn. Spring run-off had eroded ruts deep into the sand. Only weeds and rubble supported the wheels of the car. We'd taken my old Chevette rather than his gold Trans-Am, and now I knew why. Fifteen miles into the bush we lost the muffler.

"At least the bears will hear us coming," I said loudly.

He grinned, but didn't deny there were bears. Instead he murmured, "Lions and Tigers and Bears, Oh my!"

I laughed at him. He thinks we're on the Yellow Brick Road! Oh my! I laughed again and joined the chant. We repeated "Lions and Tigers and Bears, Oh my!" louder each time until we bellowed over the rattle of my car.

We reached the cabin, our voices hoarse, our ears strained.

"Poor Baby," I said touching the mud-caked fender. "Do you think we'll get back out?" But he was already striding toward the cabin.

He stopped and looked back at me. "I want you to know this is my special place. I wouldn't bring just anyone here. I want you to appreciate the honour."

I nodded. He pivoted on his toes. He held his face in a generous smile as he circled the cabin once. His body moved with an easy grace, forgoing his usual strut. He walked around the cabin twice, singing quietly to himself, his hand caressing knots and scars in the cabin's wood.

Years worth of human litter lay everywhere around

the shack. Plastic bags and beer cans were scattered in the underbrush. An old stuffed sofa rotted in front of the cabin. I wondered what lived in that couch. Moose carcasses had hung to bleed from a cross-beam nailed between two trees, not eight feet from the cabin door. Perhaps the hunters sat on the sofa to have a beer while they admired their handiwork. Even the trees between the cabin and the small lake it overlooked had been slaughtered, the logs left to rot.

"I used to come here with my old man," the Alley Cat said as he slipped his hand under my jacket, under my sweater to the skin on my back. "My sisters and mother never came here."

He opened the cabin shutters then flung open the unlocked door. We walked inside, billows of dust rising with our feet. In the one big room two armchairs, their upholstery split, huddled by an iron stove. A counter, table and sink formed a mock kitchen at one end. Cobwebs drifted on the breeze from the open door. Mice scattered. A hand-drawn map noting the location and history of kills decorated the cabin's kitchen wall. By the window naked Marilyn Munroe look-alikes, one holding mistletoe and wearing a Santa Claus hat and red high heels, another raising her arms to stroke rabbit ears above her head, advertised Sure Shot buckshot.

I worked inside the cabin. I brought in the food and clothes from the car and organized them, cooked, swept, and cleaned up after the mice and spiders. Outside, he collected some wood from the spoiled scenery. At least we could burn the wood the hunters had left.

Late in the afternoon we sat in the open window and shot a hand-gun at discarded beer cans. The sights skewed off to the right, making it impossible for me to fire with any accuracy. He took great pride in his ability to win at games. He could out shoot me, out throw me in darts and out play me in chess. I hate games.

Time passed slowly. He straddled the cabin window sill and ate a whole watermelon. The pink juice rolled down his face; the back of his hand rubbed it into his pores with satisfaction. He spat seeds with exaggerated drool. I watched him once take a black head out of a pore on his face with a straight pin. As he sat there and ate and spat and slobbered and gloated over the sweet pink flesh of the watermelon, I could think of nothing but that pin and that infected pore.

To avoid the gluttony in the window, I turned my attention to myself. For two hours I sat at the rough lumber table, easing ceramic salt and pepper shakers. I arranged and rearranged them, moving the tall yellow cylinder of pepper a centimetre, then the white sphere of salt.

I pictured my father in our kitchen, grinning with his hand over the telephone receiver. "She wants to know how I got my daffodils to bloom so early." It was late in March. I was thirteen.

"I'll be happy to tell you, Marie. Come over and have a good look," he said into the phone. He hung up.

"Come on," he said, "I got one on the line."

My father and I pulled on our coats and stood in the snow waiting for Marie Wilkinson to join us from across the street.

Marie bent over the mound of snow that covered our garden and stared at my father's flowers. Yellow plastic daffodils.

"Damn, you got me again," she laughed.

The dot of light high on the curve of the salt shaker

reflected the cabin in its glaze as in a fish-eye lens. I eclipsed the spot of light with the pepper and delighted in its shadow.

I remembered my father, when I was about sixteen, sitting in his rust-coloured La-Z-Boy hunched, his head in his hand. After four hours, I asked him if he was all right. He didn't answer. My brothers stayed away from the house. Mom spent a lot of time in the kitchen.

A day later I bought a black eight-week-old puppy from a neighbour. Mom named him Manfred the Wonder Dog. I heard Mom talking to Manfred on the stairs: "Who's my sweet baby? Who's my good boy?"

Dad didn't move from his chair, didn't talk for three days. His face crumpled in strain lines between his brows. He stroked his cowlick and kept his eyes down. That's when I first saw his depression. It lasted for ten years sometimes fading but always present.

I don't want to be like Dad.

I placed the cylinder on its side then drew rings in the spilt black pepper.

My nose tingled and I felt tears swelling in my eyes. My stomach knotted.

I waited with my mother in a cold Ottawa East Hospital ward during my father's emergency surgery. Mom looked old. She trembled and stared out the window. I stared at her. A minister, a family friend, walked slowly into the room his face drawn, his eyes sore. My stomach lurched. I said, "I can't take this," and bolted. I thought my father had died. He survived that operation and died years later.

I have the power here. I have perception and will. When I go to the operating room on Tuesday, the surgeons will change my body, but I'm going to make it work. Me. Just me.

The Alley Cat circled me. "What the hell are you doing?"

"Thinking."

He sniffed, picked up the salt and pepper shakers and ambled to the window.

"Are you going to tell me if you were fucking Nicole the other night?"

"I'm not going to tell you anything now. I told you already I have something to tell you, but not until you're out of the hospital."

"What difference does it make before or after surgery? Tell me now. I want to know."

"NO." The Alley Cat pulled a torn raincoat off the armchair and shoved his arm through the sleeve.

"We're going for a walk," he ordered.

I felt agitated, so I went. We walked through the rain in silence. The rain fell cold and windless. The air smelled delicate, the woods new-born. I knew the hospital promised only the smell of unbathed ill bodies filled with medication, or disinfectants and harsh cleansers. I filled my lungs and nose with the fertile musky scent of spring.

"There were fresh marks on the cabin by the door. What were they?" I broke the silence.

"There are lots about stories of male bears being attracted by human poontang. I suppose that's it," he said.

I blinked at him. He gawked at me.

"Poontang. You know, tastes like chicken, smells like fish."

I blinked again. He peered at me in disbelief.

"You weren't kidding about being a minister's daughter, were you?" he said. "Little man in a boat?"

I made no response. He tossed a gesture at my groin. Dumbfounded, I continued to stare at him.

"Your sex, Sweetie, it smells. Bears like it too." He walked on ahead.

I dropped my head and trudged along, struggling to keep up with his pace.

How can a man who reeks like rancid fat tell me that I smell like a fish? I thought. "I don't smell like a fish!" I said when I caught up to him.

"Forget it." He turned his back to me and continued ahead, in an ancient rumpled Nor'wester patched with silver gaffer's tape, armed with a staff and a wild grin. He looked like Lord Baden-Powell gone mad. I liked the image and tried to amuse myself with it but couldn't sustain it. I felt stupid. What the hell am I doing out in the woods with a man like this?

Out in the mist and the tender new green, pretending to harvest the bowed curls of fiddleheads, I became excited at the prospect of summer expanding in front of me. Heat rising and billowing under flowing summer skirts, the colour and cloth sticking to my ileostomy-freed belly. A belly again flat and beautiful, a single lean line. Even now, in early May, the heat of the plastic bag against my skin annoyed me. In the summer, baby powder applied three times a day to the skin under my ostomy bag would neither keep my mind off my belly nor my skin cool.

I'll be pretty again. I'll be strong. I'll be sexy again.

I watched the rangy, masculine figure pick his way through the bush, stalking a moose by its droppings in the mist.

"Yes," I told myself and hurried to catch up with him.

"I want to rut." I said evenly.

"What?"

"You know. Rut." I let the R and the T roll on my tongue. "Forget the moose, put your ass up against the tree."

"What's got into you?"

"I'm going into the hospital soon, remember?" I stared back at his green eyes. "I want to feel it all now. I won't be able to have sex for weeks after surgery. I want it now." I knew from my reading that pelvic surgery could leave me with nerve damage that lessened or removed the sensations of sex, but I didn't tell him that. The less he knew of my thoughts the better.

So we did it, outdoors, in the rain and the mud and the moose droppings. His rhythm was as relentless and predictable as a drum machine, as devoid of nuance as bad pop music, lacking improvisation or warmth but filling the spaces with entertainment that demanded no thought. Beat, bop, cliché. I took comfort in his impersonality, didn't care that it wasn't love. I felt life in my pelvis, in my heart moving my blood and in the cold air on my lower back. I could get pleasure from my body, not just the pain that awaited me.

As I made myself climax, I screamed into the woods, "Jesus Christ where are you?"

He shook me by my shoulders and said, "Right here. Right here. What's the matter?"

"Not you, you idiot!" I shoved hard against his chest.

"You're not getting weird on me, are you?" he growled back.

"I'm frightened. I haven't put on enough weight. I need to put on more weight before surgery. I want my ileostomy closed, but I don't want the pain it'll take to do it. There's not enough time. Christ. What am I going to do? There's not enough time." Panic rose in my voice.

"Okay," he said, "Okay. Let's go back to the cabin. I'm cold anyway. It's getting dark. Put your pants on. We'll go back and eat. Let's go."

We arrived back at the cabin five minutes before darkness fell. He built a fire in the stove and drank gin while I ate and ate and ate. I had ten pounds to gain and precious little time to do it. Surgery waited just three days away and the heavier I went in the better my chances for a quick recovery. He got drunk early that night. We had sex as he ordered it.

The next morning I awoke first. Outside the wind blew cold and rain tapped the window slightly. The Alley Cat had erected a domed tent in a corner of the cabin. He said our body heat would be better used and the tent would keep the mice at bay. I lay still, locked in his grip, staring at the orange nylon above me. His sweaty body stuck to mine. He lay asleep and naked. I wore cotton briefs and a T-shirt, not able to keep my thin body warm. As I moved my hand down to check my bag, his hold constricted around me.

"I have to get up," I whispered. He moaned and lifted a heavy arm from across my chest.

Quietly I got up into the cold. Quickly, I pulled on his gray woollen work-socks and the closest sweat-shirt, unzipped the tent and stepped out into the cabin.

The fire's out. I crossed the cabin watching mice scurry. My trespassing must frighten them.

The dark and chill of the early morning rain invited me to dump the contents of my ileostomy indoors. I dipped a plastic cup into a pail of lake water we kept in the kitchen, perched myself on the cold white enamel of the sink and emptied myself into it. My thin stool mingled with droppings the mice had left in the sink overnight. I examined it before rinsing it away with lake water. Bits of undigested cauliflower and broccoli retained their original shape and colour on the white enamel.

I should chew more.

I flexed my sphincter muscle and tried to feel the pelvic pouch behind it but felt nothing. I relaxed and flexed again, an exercise the Prophet had told me to repeat several times a day. How will I know when to empty the pouch if I can't feel it?

I dumped a cup of lake water over the brown, away from the white, and chased it down with bleach. The sink was only a pretence at plumbing. The drainpipe ended underneath the cabin.

I crossed the floor back toward the wood stove, put on a garden-glove, flung open the iron door and examined the fire. To the embers I added kindling, blew gently and teased them back to life. Flames rose. When they threatened to consume the twigs with a flash, I fed in logs until the fire roared and crackled with satisfaction. I provided a last great log to feed the fire through the next few hours. As the flames licked at the edges of the log I thought about bolstering myself with food. In anticipation of the post-surgical weight and energy loss, I tried to build an armoury of fat. I studied the flames a moment longer then went back to bed. The Alley Cat lay awake stretched out on his back, his hands behind his head.

"Glad to see the fire, at least, is getting some attention."

"Roll over. Let me see your back."

A strange ritual had developed between us. He'd lie on his belly and I'd rub and pinch and pick at the pimples and black heads on his back. He turned over and I mounted the hollow of his broad back.

"I've never had a lover who paid so much consideration to my body, and so little attention to my cock," he said.

I lay down beside him. Silence. I made a habit of silence. I cultivated it. I sat and listened, held myself stiff and tight, my face expressionless. Often I wondered if I'd ever feel anything other than silence, lust or anger for him.

After several minutes he said, "What do you think of my citadel of love?"

"You mean the tent?"

"Yeah."

"It is very nice," I said, and in my head began preparations for breakfast.

"What! Is that all?" He rose slightly. "NICE?"

"Okay. It's a fine tent, a wonderful tent, a grand tent."

"Come on now, it's better than that!" he nudged me with his shoulder.

I propped myself up on my elbows and gazed around theatrically. "The best tent in Canada!"

"You can do better than that."

I gestured operatically. "The best in all the world."

"What about the cosmos?"

"I've never been in the cosmos," I rolled to my side and watched him.

"What about astro-projection?"

"Yeah, but I was travelling without a tent."

"But there must have been other tents out there to compare this to."

"Okay, okay, this is the best tent in the cosmos." I nodded to him.

"Just the cosmos?"

"How about the best tent in any space, any time, in any culture?" I laughed.

"Why are you limiting it to time, space and culture?"

I took a breath: "The best tent ever conceived by any form of intelligent energy, beyond the confines of time, space and imagination!"

He slapped my thigh. "Aw, come on. You're exaggerating!" He rolled over, consumed by his own laughter. I laughed a little at him but only a little.

I washed and peeled apples and bananas for breakfast while he collapsed the tent. Before he ate, I had finished my fruit and loaded the car. He chewed slowly.

With the car door open, sitting in the driver's seat I calculated our time of arrival in Toronto and my arrival at Toronto Memorial the following day, Monday. Surgery, Tuesday. After surgery, my ileostomy closed, the summer beckoned. The Prophet had assured me this surgery would be different — only 45 minutes, less pain, less blood loss, less recovery time.

I just want it done. I just want to go. The Alley Cat and whether or not he fucked Nicole doesn't matter; only surgery matters.

"The gun, where is it?" he called from the cabin door.

"How the hell should I know? You packed it. It's your damned toy not mine! Hurry up, will you?"

He curled his spine in a long slow arch and checked his shoe laces.

"Don't be such a child," I yelled.

"I'd be more careful what you say," he said in the low tone he liked to practice. "I'm the one who knows the way out, remember?"

I waited, angry but silent.

We stopped in Mattawa, filled the gas tank and used a restaurant washroom. We headed toward Toronto in silence. The car didn't have a tape deck and we didn't talk. At Lake Nipissing we stopped at an elevated gravel parking lot with lavatories, a lookout. Lake Nipissing, vast and brilliant in the reflected sun, abruptly parted the dense forest. I wished I could change places with the lake. I wished I could live forever.

The air was unusually warm and gentle for May, but a breeze bellowed up the cliff off the lake. Caught in the upward current, a seagull with a wire hanging from its claw screamed and soared toward us.

"Where's the hand-gun?" I asked.

"Why?" said the Alley Cat.

"I'm going to shoot that bird. The wire is embedded in its claw. Can't you hear the pain? I want to stop its pain. I'm going to shoot it," I said.

"It's two o'clock and three hundred and thirty clicks to T.O." he said. "There's too many people around. Forget the damned bird."

He got in the car behind the wheel. I pondered the screaming gull. Torture, I thought, but got in the car, and we drove.

At 140 kph. my car knocked with effort and slid as the highway curved to an extended downhill bank.

"You're going too fast. The car won't take it."

"Speed limits are made by asshole politicians who live in the city and don't know how big this country is."

"Where'd you say you were from sailor?"

"You'd call it a lunch bucket town — St. Catharines."

"All you guys from St. Catharines think you're from the country. You think St.Catharines is like all of Canada. Well, it's not. It's the industrial heartland. One of the easiest climates in Canada. My husband came from St. Catharines too." I said, my voice unusually loud.

He faked a yawn. "Yeah, what high school did he go to?"

"I didn't think you made it as far as high school."

He stayed silent for several miles. I watched the trees whiz past and counted the cars ahead of us when a stretch of highway opened.

"When I first took you on," the Alley Cat said without looking at me, "I thought since you were divorced you'd know about sex, but I'd only score you a six out of ten. Not up to my usual standards. I'll have to teach you some new moves." He glanced at the rear-view mirror, then at me. "Next time I'll tie you down naked to that big table in the cabin and keep out of your line of sight, so you'll never know when I'm coming in for you."

"Why would you do that?"

"Other women like it. What's the matter with you? Think I'd leave you there? Don't you trust me?"

"I'm supposed to prove I trust you by letting you terrorize me? Are you crazy? I'll be strapped down enough in the hospital, thanks."

"Yeah but this will be pleasure."

"Yeah, your pleasure — your fucking power pleasure. Forget it. There won't be a next time." I took care not to raise my voice.

"Okay," he said and glared at me. "You want to know what's what. Nicole is pregnant. She's due before Christmas."

"Congratulations."

PATIENT CLINICAL REPORT
Toronto Memorial Hospital

Patient's Name	D.O.B.	Room No.
Carr, Robin	14/02/58	ES09-411

Service	Referred by	Rept. date
Coleman, M.	Dr. J. Axon	D-22/05/87
Gen. Surgery		T-27/05/87

OPERATIVE NOTE

Operation: Closure of loop Ileostomy

Date of Operation:	22/05/87
Staff Surgeon In Charge:	Dr. M. Coleman
Assistant:	Dr. R. MacDonald/ Dr. S. Khamis
Anaesthetist:	
Anesthetic:	General endotracheal
Preoperative Diagnosis:	Loop Ileostomy/Papilla pouch

History:

This is a 29 year old white female well known to our hospital. Post pelvic pouch procedure in the past with anastomotic complications, who underwent repair and was admitted on this occasion for loop ileostomy closure after a negative barium pouchogram.

Procedure:

Blood loss: None
Packs: None
Drains: None
Sponge and instrument counts were reported as correct x 2
Complications: None

After adequate induction of general endotracheal anaesthesia, the patient was prepared and draped in the supine position.

The right lower quadrant ileostomy was mobilized at the mucocutaneous junction down to the fascia. The proximal and distal loops were mobilized from the abdomen and delivered through the wound. The loop ileostomy was a loop end ileostomy with a staple line across the distal limb. The ileostomy was descensus upon itself.

The distal loop was opened from a small opening at the corner. The GIA staple line was passed down the antemesenteric surface of both limbs. The limbs were brought together and the instrument was fired, creating a side-to-side anastomosis. The TA55 stapler with 4.5 staples was placed across the end, separating the GIA staple line and fired to create a functional interrupted sutures of 3-0 Vicryl. Hemostasis was accomplished with electrocautery and a 3-0 chromic stitch on the staple line within the bowel lumen.

The intestine was replaced into the abdomen after opening the upper portion of the fascia slightly to facilitate replacement. The stomal site was then closed with a layer of No.1 figure-of-8 Dexon and two 3-0 Dermalon skin sutures. A sterile dressing was applied.

The patient was returned to the Recovery Room awake and alert, having tolerated the procedure well.

Dr. S. Khamis   SK/dl

In The Abattoir

Linda, the head cheerleader, refuses to pair off with me. She poses, hand upon her tilted hip, her long blond hair freshly curled, her beige skin even and lovely, staring at me. She looks as plastic and bloodless as a Barbie Doll.

"You told me you have arthritis," she says.

"I do. In my hands. But it's not bad now. I want to play." I hold out my hands to show their fitness.

"Well, I don't want to get it."

"Get what?" I ask, mystified. She nods to my out-stretched hands. My gesture changes to a plea. "You can't get arthritis," I pause then add, "at least not from casual contact!"

"How did you get it then?"

My heart sinks. My hands drop.

"It's a side-effect of my disease," I confess.

Linda The Cheerleader, sniffs and glares at me as if she has caught me in a lie. I wonder if she recognizes me.

Then we become our nine-year-old selves, Brownie uniforms, knee-socks, pixie cuts and freckles.

"But Linda, we went to camp together."

Linda flashes eighteen again. She lifts a manicured hand off her hip and flicks her fingers toward my abdomen. "Well I really don't want to get that!" Linda says.

"You can't get it. It's an hereditary disease. My father

died from a similar one. I got it from his side of the family. It's not my fault."

"You're dirty," Linda says.

Now I understand.

"Just stay away from me." She holds her position and waits for my response. I heave a basketball toward her, displaying what an expert partner she is passing up, but she makes no move to catch it. The contaminated ball bounces in ever decreasing arcs, her eyes following until it halts. I lurch and feel vomit clog my throat. Beads of perspiration drench my hair-line. I escape the basketball court and find myself outside, behind the school.

I circle the track pounding the tarmac with my feet. I weep, curse, and run and run and run, but Linda just stands there, watching.

My leg muscle contracted and I jolted awake. My back, soaked with sweat, clung to the bed clothes. I lifted my head slightly off the pillow to assure myself the nightmare had gone. Around the ward I heard the sounds of ill people sleeping. Moans and sighs through the mist of sleep and drugs rose from the other three beds like loon calls on a lake in early morning, chilling then comforting. I tried to imagine myself in a canoe on still water, a quiet glide over the surface. I tried to make their sighs into familiar wilderness but couldn't manage the transformation. Three older women were shifting in their sleep, rolling over in their pain with careful motions limited by tubes and drugs. I lay still and listened, forewarned by the just-passed spasm that pain floated not far away, awaiting my next blunder.

I remembered the panic I felt after my first surgery when my husband left after visiting hours and I was alone all night. Unprotected, alone and lost in the woods.

Even after I had returned home and slept in the same bed as Joseph, I put a pillow over my belly and clutched it all night so they couldn't come and open me in my sleep.

Anticipating the pain, I rolled to my side then lingered and waited for the constriction to release. My skin tingled with fever. I stroked my abdomen: no bag, just a gauze dressing where it used to be. Three days earlier, an hour-long operation closed my ileostomy.

I measured the distance to the phone with my eyes before I risked the stretch to the five or six centimetre incision. I managed the reach. It was early, still dark, but he had to be up shortly anyway. He answered softly, slumber fresh and deep in his voice.

"Hi, Beautiful," he cooed.

My throat burned, raw and swollen from the tube pushed down it during surgery. My voice rasped. I hoped my breathlessness sounded sexy, not feeble. A strange yellow energy charged the ward. I felt the other sleeping women were listening, perhaps recognizing not the words but the murmur of a woman to her lover in the early morning. I wondered if he would find me more pleasing without my ileostomy.

Victor, one of three male nurses on the surgical ward, appeared to push a needle in my hip. I curled to my side, tossed back my covers to reveal my buttocks to him. My hips bulged, dotted with scabs and tiny blue bruises from being punctured every three hours. Victor roughly pinched a swollen mound of flesh with one hand and aiming the needle with his fist, jabbed me. Victor never injected softly — he said he didn't want me to like it too much — but he always showed up with my dope before the shift changed. I appreciated that he remembered.

His milky skin and dour manner reminded me so much of my Grandmother Carr that I secretly called him Mildred.

"Thanks." I covered myself and turned on my back.

"Rub it hard. It'll work better," he said checking my I.V.

"How do you feel?" He focused his eyes hard on me. "I hear you've been having trouble evacuating your pelvic pouch."

"Happy to be finally closed."

Mildred's fifty-year-old face sagged with fatigue from another demanding twelve-hour night-shift in this and other rooms.

"Grand," he said and crossed the ward.

I recognized all the nurses by name, but it provided shallow comfort. They knew about me. They remembered I was married when I first came here. The Prophet's assistant told them I wasn't now. When my mother visited she told them my father died of intestinal cancer. She told them about my two brothers. When Lucy visited, she told them about my work, about the university's lay-offs and how I might lose my job. The accumulated information gave them the right to ask me questions as if their good intentions provided solace. I saw only cold, hell-paving charity. They used me as an example of Things Could Be Worse when other patients annoyed them. Such are the rules of the abattoir: use what ever helps to survive the moment. Pain passes, but its passage can be assisted. My father taught me that.

Mildred carried his tray of needles to the woman whose bed lay diagonal to mine. She'd had emergency gallbladder surgery two days ago. The first day post-op, despite Mildred's insistence, she refused to help herself.

She refused to stand and walk. I'd learned the sooner you met the pain, the sooner it left. Movement was essential. I knew the second day always dawned harsher. Less anesthetic remained in the body to cushion it. More consciousness cleared the head to feel more pain. The longer you waited the more difficult moving became.

Horror, surprise and fear welled on the second day. Last night the gallbladder patient whined and snivelled before the devil pain. Mildred soothed her with drugs and talk most of the night. At 5 a.m., exasperated, he pointed across the gloomy ward at my bed.

"You see that girl over there, she's in here all the time. You're in pain now but there are other people on this floor that will have pain for a lifetime. This floor is full of people having intestinal surgery. Gallbladder surgery is ..." He picked up his tray of medications. "I've got people in worse shape than you to see to."

As Mildred left the ward he threw me a glance. I remembered no gauge, no thermometer, existed for pain. How did they know who felt more pain? Yet I nodded my head to Mildred in acknowledgement. That woman was a rookie. Any veteran expected pain. I thought of pain as a force all its own. It lived and fed in hospitals, but it could follow you home, extorting submission like dues before you moved on. It couldn't be conquered, only appeased. When cancer teemed in my father's spine, not even morphine delivered to his blood stream drop-by-drop through a pump installed in his neck could ease his pain.

I felt the first touch of my painkiller. Things Could be Worse. As I lay there and waited for the painkiller's embrace, I thought about my father, the ripe light of summer dusk in Ottawa. Gordon was fourteen, Alan eight. We shot baskets with our father in the driveway. I was ten and my father, although he stood only five-foot-nine, still seemed tall. He seemed invincible. As I dribbled past him, just brushing his shirt-sleeve, my father tumbled to the pavement.

"Foul!" Gordon screamed.

"I barely touched you." I yelled as I gazed down at my father's sprawl on the black driveway.

"That's right, but the ref doesn't know that." My father grinned up at me. He stood, took the basketball from me, aimed and sank it from centre court.

My father caught the rebound, then handed me the ball."I'm sure Gordon already knows this. You try."

I dodged him, bounced my way under the net. As I leapt for the basket my father grabbed the cuff of my shorts and lightly tugged down. My brothers laughed as my shot ricocheted. My ears burned.

"If you do it correctly the ref will never see it," my father said. "Your mother will disagree, but there are times it doesn't pay to be an innocent. Know the game." He smiled and passed me the ball again.

The night my father died, as I sat in his hospital room, I thought about our basketball lessons. I expected him to, I wanted him to, jump up and say "Here's the trick!" But he lay there dying. That shell, its mouth open and gurgling, was not my father. His body simply continued running out of habit. It stopped a few hours after I saw him. The dying isn't hard; it's getting there that is.

I drifted in darkened self-absorption. Just me. I am enough. The distance between my mind and my body expanded as the demerol drifted through my blood stream. I existed only faintly, as a receptor. Painkillers don't kill pain. They just made me not give a damn. I watched my body, pitied it, sat whole long, long days by a window as my mind strayed. No judgement. No choices. Just watching. No obligations. Trapped and free at the same time. Just me. Only me.

I sat encased, engrossed in myself. The metal taste stuck on my tongue though I hadn't eaten or drunk for days. I didn't care if I ever ate again. I felt my body had turned inside out, nerves, guts, sinuses exposed. My arms, hands, feet could smell. My veins could taste. Smell and taste gushed through a needle attached to a bag of solution suspended from a pole. I hung suspended like the bag on the I.V. pole that fed me. The chemical reaction between the painkillers and the liquid pouring into my veins controlled my moods. I could time my downs, anticipate my highs. Clear sacks of saline combined with demerol sent me on a high. A yellow bag of potassium solution injected with antibiotics meant I had a minute to brace myself against despair. Nothing I could do stopped the darkness. I just had to wait. That's why they refer to us as patients.

I found myself seated by a hall window. I had no memory of how I got there, but it didn't matter. I could barely distinguish where my body ended and the chair began, couldn't find the parameters of my head. Demerol and I had turned a corner, crossed a threshold into sweetened mellowness. I sat. I found a walkman plugged into my ears. Mary Margaret O'Hara sang. Clouds sailed, slow bellowing puffs outside the hospital window. Sun blazed on a jet's wing. Colour danced. Music filled everything. My senses were my whole mission. I just existed. That's all.

Then pain broke through the artificial bliss and kicked me from the inside, hurled me down the stairs and stomped on me, but I didn't panic. I remembered pain wouldn't kill me, knew not to waste energy being frightened of it, knew not to try and move away from it.

Just breathe. Concentrate: in through the nose, out through the mouth. Control what you can. You can breathe, just do it. Feel the cold air coming in then the warm air passing out. In. Out. All pain passes. Breathe and wait. In. Out. It's going to hurt, but if you don't get back to your bed it will hurt more. Stand up. Walk.

I shuffled, doubled over, clutching the hall banister.

A nurse saw me. I watched her eyebrows lift and her forehead crease.

"I'll bring you a shot," she said and ran off.

I got back to my bed, I don't know how.

The intercom cried, "Keys to the desk" and the narcotic cabinet opened for me.

The injection dropped me into sleep.

It's so big in my body and I am so small within it. I wander from room to room as if in a gallery. So many things to see in here. So many things I feel I should know but don't. So much space in here. It's hard to believe there's only me in here. I can't feel my feet. Where are they? Where are my kidneys? My bowel is gone; has everything else shifted?

A dark museum. Huge red inflamed pimple-like forms spotted my belly. The museum's curators come around to inspect me, but they don't know what to do. They can't figure out how to enter me into their collection. They don't talk to me. I can't make them hear me. I'm just something they put in a vault. But I want to understand the growths so I start clawing at them. One head bursts and unfurls a long white-scaled tendril of rotting, stinking, moving cells, ulcerous and festered and attached to my belly. I take a deep breath and yank it off. I see myself writhing.

I wake to the Prophet in his white lab-coat over his surgical greens, touching my shoulder, gazing down at me. Interns stand behind him like a choir. I concentrate, focus my vision only on the Prophet.

Surgery failed. The pouch leaked inside me. Shit floated free in my abdomen. Septic shock, he said. I didn't understand. I felt myself sink in cold clammy mud, nothing to hold on to. Pain dragged my head under the surface, tried to suffocate me. I might drown in my own internal waste. There is nothing they can do, he was saying. Nothing but wait. Too toxic to withstand surgery, so toxic I threaten infecting the surgeons as well. Nothing they can do, he said.

I submerged again, my eyes heavy with mud. I heard my voice once in a while, but nothing else. Outside they touched me, injected me, drew blood samples, but I felt nothing. They spoke to me but I heard nothing. Just me. Only me. Breath, but no control over it. Not now. No. Not now. I won't. I worked too hard to get to this surgery. NO. My voice died.

My body lay curled, tainted green and angry, my hand clenched in a fist in front of my face. Friends visited and said goodbye. My mother sat by my bed twelve hours a day reading, knitting, waiting. I knew nothing of this. Lucy told me weeks later. I only knew my rage.

Two days passed. The nurses came and went and took my vital signs every 15 minutes. The pinch of the blood pressure cuff on my arm annoyed me. The wheeze as it pumped up irritated me.

"Why are you doing that so often?" I heard my own voice.

"You've been away."

"Oh yeah," I replied with my eyes closed. "Cathy is that you?"

"I'm glad you're back."

I pried my heavy eyes open and peered around the room. Dark blue walls crowded my bed. "What am I doing in a private room?"

"They moved you a few days ago. I better go get a doctor." Cathy paused and touched my shoulder. "Your mother just left. She's very upset."

A doctor whose voice I didn't recognize came in.

"How are you?" he asked politely, almost reverently.

"I'm okay," I said. I always said that. Sounds like me, I thought. "What time is it?"

He laughed, "About 10 p.m." He hesitated then said, "We have a ninety-percent success rate with pelvic pouches. I'm sorry you've turned out to be one of the ten percent. Coleman will be in to see you in a couple of days. Rest now."

Within a couple of days I could sit up by myself, but a stutter punctuated my speech. My voice whispered. I spoke very little. It was difficult and tiresome to make myself understood. Why speak? Words couldn't change the failed surgery.

Closure hadn't worked. It was out of my control. It didn't matter how much I wanted it, I couldn't have it. I would have an ileostomy forever.

Technicians drew blood samples from my hand. Nurses recorded my vital signs. My I.V. dripped. During those two days I lay still and silent, thinking. I am here to be punished. Hospitals are places where they put people to punish them for being ill. When they decide you have been punished enough they let you go. Healing has nothing to do with it. There's nothing left. My father's gone. My marriage is gone. My health is gone. My looks gone. Give me a place to hide and I'll gladly hide. My life is small, worthless. I belong in the abattoir.

The Prophet arrived unaccompanied on the third evening as the light in my private room faded to shadow.

"We're going to give you a temporary ileostomy until you're in better shape. You're not stable enough now. We'll bring you back to the hospital in a few months to extract the pelvic pouch."

I turned my head away from him.

The Prophet sat by my feet, on the bed.

"Robin, this will be an important surgery. How you feel going into it will influence the outcome." He paused. "If you're so depressed that you won't fight, I'll wait. But you'll have to stay in the hospital." The Prophet waited, but I kept silent. "Robin. What do you think Robin?"

"It's sexier to be healthy with an ostomy than sick with a pelvic pouch," I said without looking at him. That's what I would say to a friend in my position, but did I believe it? The next morning they took me down to the O.R. suspended on a bed of nylon rope. My thick chart balanced at the foot of the stretcher.

In the familiar cold, green room, people in green surgical gowns and plastic shower caps scurried like mice. The gowns were green to relieve eye strain from focusing on the red of surgery. The staff paid little attention to me. For them, my seventh surgery meant just another duty in another routine day. A woman with a practised gentle voice came over to me and asked my name. Two nurses wearing surgical masks transferred me to a narrow, hard, high table. Intense light shone from a chrome-lined concave disk above the table. I noticed the instruments laid out in order, parallel, equal distance between each steel tool. A nurse told me to slip my arms out of my gown, so I lay on the table almost nude in a room full of strangers. They affixed adhesive circles to my chest and back and side to monitor my heart. They put a clamp on my finger to detect the proportion of oxygen in my blood. They said they were ready, bound my arms by my sides and told me to count backwards from 100.

General anesthetic is not a gentle slide beneath the surface of consciousness. It's more like drowning. My mind kicked and fought for control as I suffocated under a weight I recognized but didn't understand. The needle — already the gauge of a knitting needle — seemed to expand when they pushed the corrosive drug into my tissues. In a heartbeat or two the anesthetic moved from my wrist to my head, burning my vein as it flowed. Then the taste came. It came up not down, rising from the back of my throat. A violent, putrid, concentrated, garlic taste. I wanted to vomit. I wanted to yell, "Don't do it," but then I was out.

I opened my eyes and lifted my head slightly. A green cloth was draped in front of me but I could see the surgeon, not the Prophet, but his associate, Dr. MacDonald. She returned my gaze and said calmly, "Hello Robin," then turning away said, "Everyone, Robin is here."

Dr. MacDonald turned back to me and said, "We're going to put you down again."

A voice called my name and I awoke flat on my back somewhere else.

"Robin," she said, "Your operation is over."

"Good," I said. I heard the nurse laugh before pain knotted my abdomen.

"Pain," I said. I tried to pull my knees to my chest to protect myself, but couldn't will my muscles to do it.

"I can't give you any more," the nurse said. "I just gave you the maximum. You'll have to wait."

I rolled my head to one side and vomited. Freshly cut muscles screeched in protest as bile rose to my mouth. It must have dribbled down my cheek, but I couldn't feel it. I felt only inside. I tried to tell myself the pain would pass but I didn't believe it. I fled up into my head, to the only safe place left, a small space behind my eyes. My eyes hadn't opened yet. I feared I would desert my body through my uncovered eyes. Beyond my head screams and moans resonated and I wondered if I had found hell. But it felt too cold, smelled too sterile.

Deep in the centre of my abdomen an icy blast swept, as though my incision enclosed the frigid operating room.

"Cold," I said.

"Okay," said a disembodied female voice.

Then warmth, as a heated blanket covered me and the cold blanket pulled away. My centre still froze.

"Thank you," I said, without assurance I was heard.

I sank again behind my closed eyes, below skinned perception.

Then came a knocking, a pounding without identification or location. A male voice spoke.

"Robin," it said. "Are you in there?"

A finger tapped relentlessly against my skull, on my forehead.

"Robin, you're not trying hard enough. You're blood

pressure is too low." The blood pressure gauge cinched my biceps.

I said, "Okay." How do I try harder? What am I supposed to do?

The hard metal clank of the straps and the click, click, clicking of the surgical lift told me the journey through long halls from the recovery room on the first floor to my ward on the ninth floor had begun.

Alone, raised metal side-rails surrounding me I touched the plastic bag. I knew without checking it was not the flat, neat, opaque, odourless type I had worn before. This appliance hung transparent, huge as a grocery bag, fastened at the bottom with a winged paperclip, fixed to my distended ileostomy by a thick rigid flange. The monstrous post-surgical bag and cumbersome flange remained for only a few days, I recalled. But I also knew it would soon release a heavy boggy smell to the sheets and room. Seven surgeries ago I wondered how anyone could live like this. I repeated to myself: It's better to be healthy with a bag, than sick with a pelvic pouch.

I lay connected to the I.V. and the catheter and the rectal tubes and the input-output charts. Life lay outside. Outside, pushing in through the needle in my vein, my body taking it in and pushing it back out. It wasn't shit, or anything nearly so reassuring or comforting that pushed out. This stuff you'd rather not see: green stomach bile and black mucus that I supposed was the anesthetic — or perhaps hell realized — leaving my body. Perhaps horror turned into black mucus when it couldn't find a way out as tears. I didn't cry. Perhaps the body did the purging when the spirit became too injured to clean itself. Red followed. Blood should be brown. Old blood, brown blood meant healing.

I lay very still and tried to find the pain. My abdomen felt hollow. I imagined the ruptured pelvic pouch inside my emaciated abdomen. I imagined a wire strung between my protruding pelvic bones, drawing them together, threatening to collapse my torso, wire coiled around frail bone like posts. It ached. In the strain, the pull between my hips, I could almost hear the high vibrating ping of the wire plucked once.

With a guarded movement I lifted my lank arm to check it with my eyes. A flat plastic tube circled my wrist with my name, date of birth and room number. An I.V. planted in my hand. Down my wrist for ten or twelve centimetres a bruise tracked an injured vein. Turning my wrist in a drugged daze, I admired the iridescent colours of my battle scar: purple, blue, green and yellow spreading and fading, the intensity of the colours transforming themselves on my wrist.

Cheap jewellery.

I.V. bags were changed. Time moved from measured fluids to the social measures of the clock and calendar. I didn't speak. I hated speaking. Not being able to control the sounds coming from my mouth overwhelmed me. Noise bombarded me.

No need to add to the general clatter of the room. Concentrate on getting out here. Deal with body now, voice later.

Absorption with my body moved from black mucus to black sweatpants in a matter of days. Athletic clothes seemed appropriate for the short walk I took twice a day, for these hikes taxed my weakened body like a marathon.

A psychiatrist came to check on me because I wasn't talking. He was a squat man with a prissy little moustache, a belly and an ill-fitting suit.

"You're depressed," he said. "I can fix that."

I blinked at him, determined not to expose my stutter.

"When you're down, go electric, I always say."

I blinked again.

"Electro-shock therapy," he said. "I've had great success with it. I can help you." He stretched out his arms grandly.

"No. Barbaric," I pronounced without a stutter. "No."

"I'll be back tomorrow," he said.

I phoned the office of the Wizard. He answered the phone himself.

"T-T-This is Robin," I said. "They want to give me sh-shock th-therapy for d-d-depression." I wasn't afraid to show the Wizard my weakness. I trusted him. I loved him. I didn't care about transference. "My stutter. I can't control it. I've stopped talking."

He bellowed on the other end of the phone. "Depression! Depression! How the hell does he expect you to feel? Is he an idiot? You've just had two radical invasive surgeries within ten days of each other! How the fuck should a person feel? Fucking shock therapy? Is he out of his fucking mind?" He shouted for me. I hadn't the energy to do it for myself. Then his voice softened. "Okay, give me his name. I'll call him and tell him to keep his hands off my patient. I'll call the surgeon too and tell him to fuck off as well. Okay?"

"Yes," I said quietly and smiled.

"The stutter," he continued, "it happens with trauma. It doesn't happen just with children. It happens to adults too. Don't beat yourself up over it. It doesn't mean you're weak. It doesn't mean you'll have it forever. Ignore it as much as you can. You have to try to talk, Robin, so they'll leave you alone. Just get yourself out of there and you and I will talk about the stutter here. I'll even take you out for lunch. You always were too thin. You must be a rake by now. It'll do me good to see you eat." He said gently, "I'll take care of the idiot psychiatrist, okay?"

"How can he be a psychiatrist?"

The Wizard laughed. "There are good plumbers and there are bad plumbers. That's all. I gotta go. I'll see you soon." He hung up.

I never had shock therapy. My walks through the halls continued. Bent over, pushing an I.V. pole in front of me past the beauty salon in the hospital lobby, I noted older women shaking their heads and talking. I felt them judging me, commenting on my posture, my emaciation, my lack of hair. I growled but dropped my head in shame. I felt pathetic. I'd overheard these comments before. I heard the judgements coming from both directions: young fashionable women's envy of my rail-like thinness, my gaunt hollow cheeks hard against jet cropped hair; and older women's distress over malnutrition. I feared extreme thinness, feared being an identifiable member of a club of sick people, yet enjoyed the envy of the chic.

Clothes became adornment and disguise. The studied imitation of health through make-up and colour and clothes could give me the power to manipulate the perceptions of others, even doctors. I didn't have to talk. Soon I never left my room without my stage make-up.

Mildred said, "When a patient reaches for her lipstick or his razor, you know they'll be fine."

After two weeks my daily walks, although wordless, became a social exercise. I joined to the slow rumble of I.V. pole wheels turning in slow circles as post-operative patients trudged round and round the corridor. Friendships grew between patients. They laughed and encouraged each other's progress.

"I see you've lost your dance partner," One patient called at another newly released from his I.V.

Their surgeries — intestinal resections, pelvic pouches, kock pouches — all seemed triumphant. I felt sure they wouldn't want to hear about my failure. I kept myself detached but nodded or waved hello as I passed.

I walked alone among the aggressive clicking of the research assistant's high heels on the hard floors and the relentless calling of the intercom, through the hissing of forced air, the haunting smell of antiseptic and the surgical lifts commuting to and from the Operating Room, everywhere the overwhelming nausea of memory.

The sixteenth day after surgery I dolled up especially for the afternoon's workout. I washed my hair and combed it carefully. I pulled a leopard-skin sweatshirt over my head and tugged my favourite black sweatpants over my bandages. The outfit pleased me. I hoped to look like myself, a character, an individual, not a patient. I lay on my bed and stared out the window, resting from the effort of dressing.

The phone rang.

"Robbie, is that you? It's Gordon." Pause. "Did I call at a bad time?"

"You're just in-interrupting my boredom."

"The kids and Susan say hello. The weather's been

terrible here and Sue's had a cold so I had to take the kids to the water slide at the West Edmonton Mall just to get them out of the house."

I moved the receiver to my other ear. "I've got the s-s-smallest violin in the w-world," I hesitated, "and I'm playing it just for you."

Click.

My face burned as I dialed long-distance for my brother. How dare he hang up.

"I'm not in here with the flu. This is my life." I spoke as loudly as I could.

"How'd you like to be on the receiving end of your sarcasm? Being sick doesn't give you free rein to be rude. I called to talk to you, to give you some company. Mom says you're not letting anyone near you. If you don't want to talk to me, fine. The choice is yours." He waited a moment then said softly, "You don't have to be so tough all the time, you know."

"I'm sorry."

"There are people who love you, but if you're going to push us away…"

"I said, I'm sorry."

I heard my brother sigh. "I'm sorry I can't be there."

"I know. I'm not s-so s-s-self-centred that I've forgotten you have a family." I paused, then spoke slower. "It's just I'm lying here all day and all I have to do is think."

"Do a cross-word puzzle or something."

"C-can't see very well." I twisted the phone cord around my finger. "I hate it here."

"I can understand that." Gordon paused. "Is Mom there?"

"Not right now." I looked at the bouquet of irises and daffodils my mother had brought me the day before.

"Robin, I don't know what's happening to you, but if you need to get mad then get mad at someone who deserves it."

"T-t-tell me, who deserves it? Me? The surgeons? Dad for being sick first? Who?" My hand tightened around the receiver.

"Get mad at God."

"I don't believe in God."

"Do me a favour and don't tell Mom that. She's counting on her prayers."

"Mom prays?"

"I guess even Dad couldn't change her Baptist up-bringing."

We both laughed.

"That's what I wanted to hear. I wanted to hear you laugh like you used to."

I felt my eyes burn. Don't cry.

"The kids are calling...I'm going to go before they wake up Sue. Take care. Bye."

I put down the phone and cried, then went to the bathroom and washed off my make-up. Maybe Gordon is right. I'll walk the halls, talk to somebody. If I don't I'll just sit here and cry all day.

I found my walkman but didn't put the headphones in my ears like usual. Small talk makes the nurses' shift pass quicker, they'll want to talk. Who cares if they can tell I've been crying. Who cares if I stutter.

On my route I walked past the nursing station. Cathy leaned against the counter, gossiping with the ward clerk. Both Cathy and I were in our late twenties, but Cathy had a plump build, a rosy complexion and disposition. I called her Chatty Cathy. She claimed her space with words as I did with silence.

"Florida," Cathy said as she leaned across the counter closer to me. "Just got back. They want Canadian nurses down there." She turned to face me. "I'm glad to see you up. We all didn't think you were going to make it. Dr.Coleman even told your mother to expect the worst. How are you?"

"I'm okay." I shifted my walkman from one hand to the other. "You've been away?" I wondered what to do next. Girlie stuff would do. I examined Cathy. "N-nice," I said as I pointed to the sun streaks her vacation had added to her hair.

She scanned the length of my body, slapped her thighs and patted her stomach. "I'd do anything to be as thin as you."

I stared at her and shook my head. I plugged my headphones in my ears and hobbled back to my room.

PATIENT CLINICAL REPORT
Toronto Memorial Hospital

Patient's Name	D.O.B.	Room No.
CARR, Robin	29 years	

Service
Dr.M.Coleman
General Surgery Service

Rept. date
Jan.5/88
Jan.7/88

OPERATION RECORD

Operation: Laparotomy, closure of loop ileostomy, resection of pelvic pouch and ileostomy

Date of Operation:	Jan 5th, 1988.
Staff Surgeon-in-Charge:	Dr. M. Coleman
Surgeon:	Dr. M. Coleman
Assistant Surgeon:	Dr. F. Albert, Dr. R. Silverstein
Anaesthetist:	
Anaesthetic:	general
Preoperative Diagnosis:	Ulcerative Colitis, dysfunctioning pelvic pouch

Postoperative Diagnosis:

Clinical Note: Robin is a 29 year old lady with a history of ulcerative colitis starting in 1981. She underwent many operations including removal of the entire colon and rectum, and she had a pelvic pouch inserted in 1985. Since then she had many problems with the pouch including leaking, fistula and pouchitis.

In the summer of this year she had an abscess which had been drained, and loop ileostomy freshened. The loop retracted and we did many pouchograms which showed leaking fistula. Accordingly, the plan was made to remove the pelvic pouch.

Procedure: With the patient in the supine position under general endotracheal anaesthesia, the abdomen was prepped and draped in the usual fashion. Through the midline scar we made our incision using electrocoagulation, going down to fascia and peritoneum. A few adhesions of the small bowel to the area of the loop ileostomy in the left lower quadrant and they were taken down easily.

Then we approached the ileostomy from outside and a second incision was made around it, about 1 1/2 to 2mm ridge of skin going down to fascia, then the ileostomy dissected from the fascia and brought intraperitoneally. The everted proximal part of the ileum straightened up and the ridge of skin excised. The loop was closed in two layers using running 3-0 vicryl sutures. After completion of this, adhesions of the small bowel down into the pelvis were dissected using sharp dissection, and the pouch was identified.

The pouch was actually stuck to the sacrum posteriorly and with some difficulty we could mobilize it. Then we dissected the pouch on the either side and anteriorly from the vagina, and this was carried down to the level of the pelvic floor. The ileum just proximal to the pouch was cleaned, and the mesentery supplying the pouch separated between Kelly forceps and ligated with 0 silk ligatures.

Then using a GIA stapler, which was applied very distally to the ileum just about 1cm proximal to the pouch, the ileum was divided and stapled in this area. After completion of this, we approached the anus from below by using the circular incision around the anus, and the dissecting posteriorly to the level of the coccyx and the levator anus muscles were separated on either side and the anal canal dissected using electrocoagulation and separated anteriorly from the vagina.

After completion of this, the pouch was removed with anus en masse. The pelvic cavity was irrigated with 3L of normal saline. Meticulous coagulative haemostasis was made.

A circular incision was made in the right lower quadrant at the area of the previous ileostomy, and this was carried down to the fascia, which was incised with cruciate incision and ileostomy incision made to the peritoneum, which allowed the passage of fingers.

The stump on the distal ileum was brought through this ileostomy incision. After completion of this the fascia in the left lower quadrant wound at the area of the loop ileostomy was closed from inside using interrupted No.1 Dexon sutures.

Then a Jackson-Pratt size 10 flat inserted into the pelvis posteriorly just in front of the scrum and brought out through a separate stab in the left lower quadrant and fixed using 0 silk suture. The midline incision was closed using running and interrupted No.1 Dexon suture for the fascia and the skin closed with metal staples.

The anterior fascia of the left lower quadrant incision was closed using interrupted No.1 Dexon sutures. A few staples were applied to close this. Then the stapler line at the distal ileum was excised and the ileum everted and fashioned using 3-0 Vicryl suture. After completion of this, dry dressing was applied to the wound, and ileostomy bag applied to the ileostomy.

First and second instrument and sponge count correct. Estimated blood loss 500 cc.

The patient tolerated the procedure well, was extubated and transferred to the Recovery Room in good condition.

The Wizard of Oz

Mom promised my father he could die at home. He stayed in the dining room. Mom removed the table and chairs, added a hospital bed, arranged the tv so he could see it, and bought a remote control. She tried to be cheerful. Visiting nurses came once a day and the air smelled like disinfectant swabs. For the first six months he got out of bed everyday, dressed and tried to walk. Mom made arrangements so someone, a friend or a neighbour, was always home with him. She feared Dad would die while she was out. Later he got up but didn't dress. As the cancer spread from his intestine to his spinal cord he stayed in bed. Any movement became painful. The nurses came twice a day. A pump administered a drop of morphine to his blood stream every few seconds. When pain grew greater than the continuous drip could handle, Mom learned how to inject more morphine.

As Dad's strength lessened and the morphine increased, neighbours and friends became less willing to visit. The thought of coming downstairs and finding him dead became more than Mom could bear. Dad moved into Ottawa East Hospital.

I felt guilty for needing attention. Raised to be a lady, educated in mannered decorum, I didn't talk to my family or my friends about the blood running daily, steadily from my rectum. I didn't mention the knotting in my abdomen or that I had to be within sprinting distance of a toilet at all times. I didn't tell anyone I had to defecate twenty times a day. Whom was I supposed to tell such rude, but painfully real things to?

Sometimes I wanted to yell, "I need help. Don't leave me alone." I never did. My pain seemed minor, a slow burn. Cancer, in my father, roared huge and immediate, an uncontrolled fire.

Joseph watched me plod toward death just like I'd watched my father. Watching is hard. But to be the one watched, to see the eyes of someone I loved bury me, was worse.

Little notice was paid to the disease growing in my gut even after diagnosis. No one wants to believe young people die of disease, so they ignore it. It appeared to alarm no one but me. The first three doctors I saw, two general practitioners, then a gastroenterologist, considered my symptoms little more than a nuisance, an inconvenience, at worst something to be endured. The specialist told me to relax, quit my job, stay home, take up a hobby. But IBD was sucking me away, allowing no food to be absorbed. Although I ate, I was starving to death. Depression settled in.

I walked alone, and mute on fine spring ice. Down on my hands and knees I tried to distribute my weight. I begged the crystallized water to support me but the ice was beyond my control. I never knew when it would give way and I would plunge into frigid still darkness; I only knew it would. Without the warmth of touch or understanding I grew colder and stiffer from lack of movement, less flexible from want of decision. Just me. Only me. And the ice.

I tried to warm my soul. I tried to battle my immobility and passivity. I tried yoga and bio-energetics, read self-help books, took twenty-five pills a day: anti-depressants, anti-inflammatories and vitamins. I became a vegetarian. I swam a mile a day to keep up my strength and continued to work. I slept eleven hours a day. Nothing helped. Inflammatory Bowel Disease is incurable, sometimes fatal. Each day passed, a gray trudge across gray ice through gray emptiness.

My marriage had been punctual but provided little comfort. At 23, after dating for four years in university, Joseph and I had glanced at each other and said "I do", like looking at a clock and eating without hunger.

I considered my options. A momentary pain to end prolonged pain seemed a good deal. I was prepared to kill myself to stop pain. I planned my escape carefully, but proud of my resolve, I did little to keep it secret.

"It'll be over soon." I told Joseph one winter morning. "You won't have to watch, don't worry, I can end it by myself."

A gentle coward, he bought me flowers rather than talk or touch me. He put daisies in a gray vase and went out for a walk by himself. The moat between us grew prettier but wider.

A month later, after our annual anti-flu shots, my husband and I sat across the desk from our family doctor.

"Tell him," my husband said in a monotone.

"I've got everything ready." I said, calmly massaging the rolling burn in my abdomen. "I'm just waiting for the right time. It'll be soon."

"What do you mean?" The physician asked as he shuffled the papers in our charts.

"The end," I said gazing at him across the cluttered

desk. "I'm going to control things. I have a bottle of scotch to celebrate. I suppose it will help with the pain too. I thought a hot bubble bath would be good. It'll make my wrist veins rise. The tub will contain the blood. I don't want to make a mess."

The physician stilled the papers, nodded and sat back in his padded black leather chair.

"I plan to tie pink ribbons in my hair. They're for him." I looked at my husband in the chair next to me. Joseph sat rigid, his hands gripping the chair's arms, his eyes fixed on the doctor. "I don't want to look too bad when he finds me. I thought the ribbons might help." Rubbing my hands together, I warmed them. "I have a bread-knife; it's sharp. I've cut myself on it before. I don't want to use anything that's his." I pointed my right hand at my husband. "I don't want him to feel responsible."

Still sitting back in his chair, the physician picked up the phone keeping his eyes locked on Joseph. He dialed and waited.

"Hello, Dr. Zuckermann? Dr.Greenberg here. I have an emergency. Can you see her this week?"

I've drunk a few bottles of scotch since then. I divorced my husband. But I'm still embarrassed about the ribbons.

Ben Zuckermann's office, the Wizard's place, the Land of Oz, had two rules: I had to be as honest as I could be and I could kill myself if I wanted, but I had to tell the Wizard before I did it. Rule two became obsolete after my first surgery. As soon as someone believed my pain was real and helped me do something about it, death became a respected opponent instead of an ally. Too stubborn to give up breathing, I figured life owed me. I'd put a lot of effort into surviving surgery; now I meant to collect. I meant to become an old woman.

I saw the Wizard twice a week for three years. A large red X on my calender marked my appointments. It took an hour on subway, bus and streetcar to commute to his office. Before surgery, I designed the route around public washrooms not efficient transfers. After surgery I adjusted the trek to avoid crowded staircases. It was never easy. Mondays at 7:30 a.m., and Thursdays at 7:15 p.m. were my regular appointments, red X's stacked like columns on the calendar grid. Now a seasoned patient, I saw him only when I wanted, usually after surgery. Control of the dates, if nothing else, was mine.

Now after my ninth surgery, I sat and waited with my cane beside me, outside the double-doored entrance to Oz. The doors to Oz hung inside an alcove, layered one upon the other, hinged on opposite sides of the frame to prevent sound leaking. A half-height wall provided a further sound barricade to the waiting room. A boxy mono-speakered clock radio — politely supplied in the trust that if the patient inside was heard, the waiting patient would switch it on — sat on a dark wood coffee table among piles of *National Geographic, Owl* and *Toronto Life*. Three matching occasional chairs, the seats and straight backs upholstered in a nubby weave of pink, gray and slate blue, pressed against three walls. Their supporting structure was dark wood, but they were light, easily moved. As I waited in one chair looking at the other two, I wondered why their positions never seemed to change.

I heard the double doors open. The Wizard's head materialized above the half-wall, his long gold hair — more fleece than hair — wild as usual. He smiled his broad grin and exposed his perfect teeth beneath soft full lips.

"Young Ms. C.!" That's how he always greeted me. "I'll be with you in a minute. I gotta make some phone calls. Wait two, three minutes then come in, will you?"

Over the phone, between patients, the Wizard operated the levers to a commercial real estate empire. He had told me many times he was a self-made millionaire. His recent acquisitions included a house on The Bridle Path and lake frontage near Bracebridge, both properties now undergoing expensive renovations.

I checked my watch and waited. After the specified amount of time I entered Oz on my cane. Beyond the double doors waited an ethereal room. No right angles, all the furniture rounded to comfort, even the walls curved gently above the cornice to meet the ten-foot-high ceiling, painted cool water-green. Tranquil colour reflected down to the room. When I lay on the taupe wool divan staring up, the room seemed to float.

Scattered over the carpet and piled in the corners was the Wizard's large collection of toys. A miniature house with mom, dad and children dolls huddled under his telephone table. An assortment of plastic animals and soft cloth puppets, little cars, a school bus with movable figures, and airplanes and trains overflowed milk crates under the window on the driveway. Against the opposite wall, a child had stacked wooden building blocks into arches and pillars. Primary-coloured modules of snap-together tracks formed a three-foot tower in the middle of the carpet. This arrangement could accommodate a competition for five marbles. He had once demonstrated the loop-de-loop, fall, jump and spin sequence he and one of his favourite children had created. Like the

Prophet, the Wizard had many child patients. Unlike the Prophet's and other medical offices, the Wizard's showed little evidence of power or authority. Without the divan, Oz could have been a friend's living room.

More than aesthetics had encouraged my love of Oz. Whatever came into my head, I had said, often with a stutter. I told him everything. Sometimes, I yelled. In Oz, the tightrope between my father's expectations of athletic tomboy independence and my mother's long-suffering tolerance broadened to a path. I walked away from my passionless marriage, my role as dutiful daughter and selfless lady. I argued with doctors, quit my respectable, but boring job at the university and had fun. The ice melted first in Oz.

The Wizard sat with his white-sneakered feet crossed atop the dark green table. Sunlight, caught in the tangle of his hair, made a soft glow around his head. I blinked at the strange halo. He cupped the phone mouthpiece, eyed my cane and said, "Just some bullshit I have to take care of. I promise it will only take a minute."

I sat down beside him and stared at the phone, a beige specimen of early push-button technology. Scotch tape held together the back right corner. Dirt, perhaps coffee but more likely cola, scummed the plastic grooves on the phone's face. The cracked plastic body was no longer secured to the electronics. The Wizard drummed and struck the green surface of the table while he shouted into the mouthpiece. I sat back and watched him like a cartoon.

The Wizard was three or four years older than me. He wore a white Oxford-cloth shirt, open at the neck, buttoned down at the collar points, sleeves rolled to just below the elbow, forearms tanned and strong. His veins bulged with oxygen. His thick body moved constantly, alternating between finger tapping and foot wagging. Beige cotton pants performed a wrinkled dance around his knees as he twitched.

Across his nose ran a scar. "I got it playing hockey," he had told me years ago when I had asked about it. I must have expressed surprise, but I don't remember saying anything. "Hah!" he had scoffed. "You think Jews don't play hockey?"

"Fine!" He whacked down the phone. "Son of a bitch!" he yelled, threw back his head and enjoyed the loud sound. He glanced at me and smiled. "Have you eaten?"

"We won't have time," I said. I hate eating, I thought.

"I've booked you for two appointments in a row. That gives us an hour and a half."

"Okay," I spoke. What is he up to? What theory is this?

I floundered but experience told me to trust his lead. I awaited his next move.

The Wizard stood and jingled his car keys in his pocket. The phone rang again. He waved in annoyance toward it. "The service will get it." He pulled on a brown leather flight-jacket and we left.

Inside his black two-seater Jaguar, I smelled the leather. I studied the intricate grain of the dashboard and wondered what type of wood. He had another car, a vintage white Mercedes convertible with a turquoise interior. This black Jag he used for business. It had the phone.

"The Mercedes?" I said.

"I had another accident. It's in the shop."

I snickered. "So what else is new?"

The Wizard ignored me.

He drove east along St. Clair, then turned south down Avenue Road. Above me, through the sun-roof, I watched the high keen February sky — sparse clouds, veined at the edges by bare black tree branches. I tilted my head level and saw the warm red of the traffic light. I turned my eyes to the Wizard.

He studied the rear-view mirror. "How's my hair?"

Over an eighteen month period, the Wizard had undergone numerous sessions to transplant plugs of hair to a barren patch of scalp. He fingered the new abundance on his head.

"You look great." He was not a handsome man but the Wizard had his charms.

I ran my hand through my own hair, habitually pushing it back though it scarcely reached my eyebrows. It was very short, cut after every surgery to camouflage its thinning. I picked a loose thread from my sleeve cuff. The scarlet wool, black velvet-collared coat and matching trousers I wore I had made myself. Pleats strategically placed gave my ileostomy room to expand. Setting the zipper in the centre back seam protected my incision from abrasion. I drafted patterns for comfort. I chose fabrics for warmth, picked colours that made me look healthier. During recuperation I had sewn entire wardrobes. When I looked in the mirror now I saw the skill I had learned, not the strength I had lost.

I slipped my hand inside my coat to hold my abdomen and recognized the vague tingle of new cells knitting in my incision.

"Where are we going?"

"A Spanish place. I made reservations. Is that okay with you?"

He has this all worked out, I thought. "Of course," I said.

"How's the eating going anyway?"

I kept my eyes on the road. "Not well," I said quietly.

"That's what I thought."

The Wizard parked his Jag. "Just a minute," he instructed. I watched the rise and fall of his body as he walked around the front of the car to open its low-slung door for me.

"Do you need help?"

"Just getting to my feet. The incision isn't closed yet. You know how to do this?"

"Are you kidding? In high school I was a hospital orderly. You ready?"

I swung my legs toward the open door, then found the pavement outside. I hooked the cane on the open door and held my arms out. He grasped my arms above the elbow, counted and pulled. I winced at the quick shift of muscle.

We slowly walked the block to the restaurant in shared silence. At the restaurant door the Wizard lightly touched my back as we entered.

Inside, the space expanded upward to a mezzanine. Rough terracotta walls broke at elegant twists of wrought-iron window. Fig trees, filled with tiny white pin lights, reached for the second floor.

The maitre d', noting my cane, directed us to an easily accessible table toward the side, on the ground floor.

"No. We'll sit there." The Wizard pointed to a secluded table at the top of the curved staircase.

"I have nothing against a little afternoon romance," the maitre d' said, beaming at the Wizard without looking at me. The Wizard nodded cordially and smiled. The maitre d' responded with a turn and led us toward the staircase.

I followed protocol. Behind the maitre d', with a little difficulty, I mounted the stairs ahead of the Wizard. I waited for the chair to be pulled out for me, the napkin to be spread upon my lap, the water glasses to be filled and the menu expounded. The waiter performed an abbreviated bow and left the Wizard and I together.

"What's with the cane, Robin?"

"I'm feeling a little vulnerable these days, but I can walk without it. It's really for other people; I mean so they leave me alone, so they won't rush me on the street or bump into me on the subway."

"Good. I was just about to launch into a litany on the trap of holding too dear a frail image of yourself." He flipped open his menu. "You'll forgive my paternalism if I order for you?"

I locked my eyebrows together: Why?

"Trust me." He grinned at me. The table shook slightly as he bounced his shoe tip off a wrought-iron bracket at its base. The Wizard twisted in the uncomfortable iron chair. After scouting the room for the waiter he said, "So what else?"

"My stutter, it's back. S-scares me."

"Why?"

I raised a single eyebrow: Come on, we both know it is commonly assumed people who stutter are either stupid or emotional wrecks.

"I think it's kind of endearing."

"Oh fuck off." I laughed but kept my body very still.

"I see you had no trouble saying that," He smiled. "You must have noticed that I stutter."

I nodded.

"Did I ever tell you how I got it?" Lightly holding his water glass at the top of its stem, he spun the ice cubes in the clear liquid.

I shook my head.

"I had this girlfriend all through medical school. I probably should have married her, but I didn't. Needless to say anyone that I would consider marrying is a good-looking, wonderful, kind, generous, gracious, multi-talented...."

I cranked my right hand: Can we get on with this?

He continued: "A lovely lady. She had a terrible speech impediment which completely encumbered her. I can assure you that she was such a terrific human being that no one would ever consider her slow-witted, yet of course she believed they did."

"As I do." I spoke softly.

"You haven't let me finish. I have a stutter. I developed it in sympathy with her. Do you think less of me?" He paused and ran his finger around and around the glass lip of the goblet. "Of course not." Another pause. Another circular caress of the glass. "Why do you think you're alone in your sensitivity?"

"Sweet story." I articulated the multiple *s* carefully.

He frowned, removed his hand from the stemware and turned his attention back to the menu.

"I brought you here to help you eat." The Wizard began an insistent rhythm with his foot.

I'll probably make a fool out of myself. I'll cry over the food or choke on it or something. I squinted my eyes at him.

"Don't worry, I'm not going to inundate you with food. Ever had tapas?" He peered over the cream-coloured parchment menu at me.

"N-no," I sputtered. The image of the Wizard as he sat on the end of my bed four years earlier, filled my head. When I told him what the surgeons had planned for me, he had cried simply, openly, briefly. From that moment forward I trusted him.

I watched his thick lips move as he said, "Well, that's what we'll have. Don't eat anything you don't want. But I'm sure you'll do all right with this stuff. Tapas are small dishes meant to be eaten with conversation. And God knows I can talk. You'll like the way they look too. Okay?"

Years ago, the night prior to my second surgery, the Wizard had sneaked in to see me after visiting hours. The boiling in my belly was excruciating. Little hope remained for my survival. Silently, privately, I was deciding whether to fight or not. Lucy and my mother spent most of the evening wringing their hands at the foot of my bed. I felt bored with sympathy. I hated feeling sorry for myself. But the Wizard wasn't empathic. He stood by my bed delivering jokes in a continuous stream, waving his hands, contorting his voice until I laughed so hard tears washed my face. The shared laughter hurt, but the cost was worth the reward: I decided to put effort into living.

I shifted my gaze from his mouth to his hazel eyes. I felt myself mesmerized by romantic fantasy. Recalling my adolescence in Ottawa, I imagined a crisp winter skate on the Rideau Canal. Frosty plumes swirl from our mouths then dissipate above our heads. My hands are blue. The Wizard opens his beaded and fringed buckskin jacket and takes my freezing hands pressing them to his warm chest. I feel his heart pound. My hands heat. I lift my mouth to his. I blinked and found myself back in the restaurant.

I'm not supposed to feel this. I don't want to feel this.

I touched my lip with my left hand. The flesh behind the middle knuckle of my middle finger I took between my front teeth. I searched my memory for perspective. I don't want to feel this, I repeated to myself; there are good reasons not to feel this.

I remembered working the Gala opening at the Festival of Canadian Fashion in the press lounge. I had spotted the Wizard in a tuxedo amid the crowd. He wore a gold lamé bow-tie and cummerbund. I couldn't believe it. The Wizard beckoned me to come see him.

"Young Ms. C!" he said. "What are you doing here?" He touched my elbow.

"What am I doing here? What are you doing here?"

An amazon in a thigh-length fitted suit jacket, a lime-green leather bra showing behind low lapels, black footless tights and a gym bag thrown over her broad shoulders strode past us. In her stiletto heels she towered more than six feet tall, greased back hair, heavy make-up. I recognized her as one of the festival models. She was perhaps seventeen, no more. The Wizard turned his head to watch the lanky giant pass.

"I love fashion," the Wizard giggled.

"Yeah, I can see that." I shot him a disapproving glance. "She's a baby."

The Wizard stepped back and looked me over. "You look fab."

I drew my elbows to my waist and bent them, hands open, palms skyward, and struck my best mannequin stance.

"And that, I like that." He pointed. Under my black

silk ottoman jacket I wore a sheer black polka-dot blouse. A three-inch translucent strip showed between the edges of my opened jacket.

A blonde man appeared beside me.

"This is my friend Sal."

Sal and I shook hands.

"Pleased," I said.

"I was just admiring her outfit, Sal," baited the Wizard.

"What's the use of wearing a blouse like that if you keep it covered up? I bet it's beautiful. Did you design it? I'd like to see the rest," Sal said.

"So would I," added the Wizard

"You spent enough time in medical school that you don't need to see my chest. You've seen plenty."

"Oh well, Sal," the Wizard snapped his fingers. "You win some, you lose some." The Wizard drew his finger along the pocket of his tux. "What d'ya think? Just had it made."

I fingered the lapel. "Nice cloth."

"Wanna try it on?"

I laughed. "You aren't going to give up, are you?"

"No." He grinned. "Here's how we'll do it. I'll count to three and we'll both take off our jackets and exchange them."

I don't know why, but I did it. On three.

I stared at the Wizard across the restaurant table. He was talking to me, something about Spain, but I wasn't listening. I noticed the expression lines around his eyes. I dropped my glance to my hands. Abruptly breaking into his sentence, I said, "Tell me again about transference."

"Why?" He knocked his index finger on the table edge.

"I think I'm in love with my psychiatrist."

The Wizard gave me a startled glance, but seeing the waiter's approach, composed his expression to order lunch.

"We'll have this and ..." The Wizard pointed at several spots on the menu.

I fondled the curl of my cane and listened to the clink of my Medic Alert bracelet as it hit the curved wood. What did I say that for? Remember he's a doctor. We are not equals. That's the agreed imbalance of seeing a doctor, any doctor. They are well and I am not. They know something I don't. I have no right to expect my love returned.

I remembered another opening gala at the Festival of Fashion. I had worked the office as a liaison between press and designers, booking interviews, directing media traffic and providing background information. The Wizard came to find me. He had worn his black wool tux, with the silk lining. But this year he had a more demure, classic black bow-tie.

"Young Ms. C. I want you to do me a favour."

"Anything."

"You think I'm a good guy, right?"

"You know I do."

"Well, there's this woman. I've been talking to her all evening. She thought I was a stand-up comic."

I studied him. The Wizard pawed at his scalp nervously. His insecurities paraded. I wondered if he might cry.

"What is it?"

"I can't believe it. She strung me along all evening,

let me buy her drinks, chatted my ear off, was real charmed — or so I thought. Then I asked if I could take her out for dinner. Not right away you understand, next week sometime." He glanced at me and laughed. "After she's had some time to reflect on what a supreme human being I am."

"Okay, what is it you want?"

He played with his fingers. He looked like a little boy.

"You want me to tell her what a great guy you are, right?"

"Yeah."

He led me by the elbow through loud posturing camps. Fashion students in drag, over-designed ball gowns, and slashed jeans and black leather, waited to be noticed. The fashion press, decked out in European classics, drank and ate around the bar. Suited business men shifted from foot to foot, amused by the show around them.

From a distance the Wizard pointed out a small woman with long pale, bottled-blonde hair. She wore a tight black leather suit, the shoulders, yoke and lapels glistening with rhinestones, sequins and ribbon flowers. As we watched she lifted her many-ringed hand and pulled at her black mascaraed eyelashes.

"I'll introduce you," the Wizard said.

We crossed the floor together.

"This a good friend of mine," The Wizard spoke to the blonde. "She's a woman of impeccable taste, and she has something to say to you on my behalf." He swept his right hand toward me like a stage cue and moved away several metres. He opened his jacket and tucked his hands into silk-edged trouser pockets. Then he lifted one hand to stroke his lip. Settling finally with his arms crossed over his chest, his feet planted firmly, he waited and watched.

I glared down at her, a good four inches taller in my heels.

"You're making a big mistake," I had said. She started to interrupt but I didn't give her a chance. "He's a wonderful and funny man. You shouldn't treat him this way." She tittered nervously and flicked her hair off her shoulder. A few strands caught on the spangles. "He's worth more than a little flirt." I glanced over at him and saw him begin a rhythm with his foot. "Leave your boyfriend. I guarantee Dr. Zuckermann is better." She looked stunned. I performed a model's pivot and sauntered toward the Wizard. He dropped his arms and waited for my approach.

"Done," I said when I reached him. He nodded. Without comment he escorted me back to the press office, pecked me quickly on the cheek and disappeared.

Across the table the Wizard was still speaking with the waiter. He didn't look like a little boy now. The Wizard looked like a man, a sensuous, intelligent man I admired despite, perhaps because of, his faults.

I felt my face blaze and scanned the restaurant for a way out of my embarrassment. I imagined flying over the mezzanine railing and escaping in an effortless swoop.

"Very good," said the waiter. He bowed shallowly, turned and left us.

"You are an extraordinary person, Robin."

"I bet you say that to all your patients."

I felt like a cat being stroked and was angry. I disliked the image. I preferred to see myself as a dog, a German Shepherd: bigger, stronger, more loyal, more demonstrative. What is he trying to do to me? I don't want to feel this.

"Not really. Some patients are more engaging than others," he said.

I read his face. He blushed too. My rage dissolved. I suppressed the urge to caress his scarlet face.

"You know how I feel about you, Robin. But if we had a social relationship, not only would I have to give up psychiatry.... Listen, it's like this: If we had a relationship outside of therapy I would get what I want and I guarantee you would not."

"So what are we doing here? We don't exactly function as patient and doctor."

"The last thing you need is more doctor domination. We like each other. Your life for the past few years has not been smooth and regular. We're close friends. I happen to be a psychiatrist and I know a great deal about you. You don't have to explain a lot of medical or emotional history to me when you get out of the hospital. Think of this, of me, as an opportunity to detox, to debrief after the hospital."

I marvelled. How does he do that? Making love without touch.

"What are you thinking?" asked the Wizard.

"Nothing seems to work. No matter how much will I exert, I don't get what I want," I said. And I want you too, I thought.

"What do you mean?"

I counted on my fingers to stress my points. "The s-surgery is a failure. The diagnosis has been changed from Ulcerative Colitis to possible Crohn's disease. But, of course they are not sure. Crohn's disease means probably more surgeries. My relationships with men are failures..."

"You had managed to convince yourself sex was love. Now that you've proven to yourself you are sexually attractive you should know better. Your husband was nice enough, more stupid than mean, but he was a wimp and your last boyfriend was a sociopath. Somehow, despite your ability to cope with other more demanding aspects of your life, you have retained your rotten taste in men."

"Including you?"

He ignored my comment and blinked five times in rapid succession. His hands, finger-nails trimmed but roughened by sport, he raised to mid-air. One finger pointed up on each hand as he found his thoughts.

"The surgery's failure is not your fault. I believe you did everything in your power to make it work. I can't imagine anyone wanting it to be a success more than you." He dropped one hand. "Which is not to say it was Dr. Coleman's fault either — though from your descriptions he could use a few sessions on the couch." Both hands rested on the table between us. "His skills as a surgeon are unsurpassed. I think you agree with me on that."

"I'm not interested in blame. It's not going to change my i-ileos-stomy or put back my large intestine." I struggled with my emotion and my tongue. I paused, mentally forming sounds, editing the difficult ones before I said them. "I just want to know if I am doing something fundamentally wrong."

"Why do you think I have the answers?" He began smoothing the azure table cloth with the palm of his hand.

Why is he making me talk so much? I summoned my most acidic voice. "We have already established that you are a psychiatrist."

"Why are you pushing me away, Robin?" He turned his palm up.

I folded my arms across my chest.

The Wizard leaned forward from his chair.

"You've put your life on hold for too long now. Not that you had much choice, given the succession of surgeries at such brief intervals. Putting all your energies into these surgeries has been important. I would have done the same thing. Now the question is: what are you going to do?"

"Go back to school," I said.

He furrowed his forehead. "What for?"

"Fashion Design."

He gave another quizzical look.

"I figure if the Prophet can redesign the body, I should be able to redesign what covers it." I snickered. "Besides, I've got the background for it."

The waiter approached, balancing a huge food-filled tray. My breath quickened.

"It's the bowls that are heavy, not the food." The Wizard beckoned the waiter. "Let her see," he instructed.

Compliantly, the waiter tipped the tray to display its load.

Thick brightly glazed blue, yellow and earthen-orange pottery bowls held small, unfamiliar arrangements of common foods. Tomatoes, sausages, mussels, rice, peppers combined in circles and ovals garnished to seduce the eye.

The waiter named each dish as he presented it.

"Chicoria con queso de cabrales," he placed a bowl

of stuffed leaves before me. "Tomates con ajo y mejorana. Salchichas frescas. Ensalada de arroz con atun." The Wizard kept his eyes averted, his voice silent, deferring as the waiter wooed me.

"Paella," whispered the dark-haired waiter, "is my personal favourite. The señorita must tell me what she thinks of it." He waited for my eyes to find his before he nodded and left.

"These are beautiful." I couldn't help but touch the rim of the nearest bowl.

The Wizard lifted a bowl and transferred a portion of fragrant multi-coloured rice to his plate. "Paella is also my favourite. Perhaps you should start with it." He invited me to take the bright bowl from his grasp.

I faltered. "It's too pretty to eat."

The Wizard waited, the bowl suspended and steaming.

I don't want to eat. It's going to hurt. So do I trust him or don't I? He's being generous. I should be gracious.

"Thank you," I said as I received the bowl.

The Wizard took my attention away from the food by talking about it, moving my attention from my mouth to my mind. Elaborately, he recounted his last trip to Spain. He set a scene and related an anecdote between mouthfuls.

"The bars in Spain where I went to eat tapas were like live theatre. It was so hot that there wasn't much to do, so Sal — you've met Sal — and I just hung out and ate. There were always lots of kids around and lots of talk."

Distractedly I ate. I watched the rise and fall of his utensils, but mostly I listened. I noted taste, texture and smell but focused on his mouth rather than my own. Gradually he turned the conversation, making me speak, first about food in general, the food before us, then the act of eating.

"I don't mind eating," I heard my voice, "in fact I like it." I was surprised by what my voice said. "But it has to be in a structured social situation. I have to feel comfortable to eat, I have to know what is going to happen, I have to trust the person I am with. Seeing people walking down the street stuffing pizza in their faces makes me nauseous. Food's not just sustenance to me anymore." Did I know that? I thought. "Eating is a privilege I may not always have."

The Wizard had a wily smile on his lips, and I knew I had been tricked. Not a cruel or devious trick, a gentle expert magic trick. I was impressed.

Dabbing blue linen at the corner of his mouth he said, "What else?"

"I can't seem to accomplish anything. It feels like an insurmountable wall. Surgery dominates my life. I don't want to believe biology is destiny, but I can't get past it. I seem so far behind everyone else because of the time I've lost being sick."

"It's not a race, Robin." He returned the linen napkin to his lap and placed his hands on the tablecloth, fingers toward me.

"All my friends have established careers or families — some measure of success. I'm tired of them feeling sorry for me. I'm tired of using my disease as an excuse."

"Listen Robin, I think you are more comfortable in your skin now than you have ever been. That is no small feat. Nor is it a feat that everyone accomplishes. The false confidence, I mean the confidence that comes to people who have large and public success in their lives, is just that, false. It's an illusion."

I stared at him.

"I know. Easy for me to say, right?"

I nodded. "I've heard all this s-stuff before. So what if I'm a nice person? Out there, beyond my circle of friends, all of whom are willing to make excuses for me because I've been sick, the big bad world doesn't care if I'm nice or not. I want a real life, not an insulated one, a life that does something, that contributes. I don't want the excuses. I don't want to define myself as a sick person."

"No. Listen to me. Life doesn't end in your late twenties. It isn't set up from birth to adulthood and then just rolls along without change. You are now, I think, the person you want to be. And a person capable of doing the things you want to do, not just the stuff you think you ought to do. Most people only do as they ought. A waste, don't you agree?"

I leaned forward, elbows on the table. "But the effect of these pep talks only lasts fifteen minutes, then I'm back on the street feeling embarrassed by my lack of status. I don't work, I don't love anyone any more. I don't produce, I just consume. I'm just a sick person, a professional patient. What good is that to anybody?"

"Love and work are, of course, important. Real important. You do love some people. You just don't currently love a man. Your experiences in the hospital, as horrible as they were, have more value than you think. You know real life. Most people don't. Most people shy away from feeling anything, from touching any strong emotion. They refuse to recognize emotion even pleasurable ones. You haven't had that option. People who have been severely ill know intimately the ordinariness and the fragility of life. Perhaps more importantly they know the real and impenetrable loneliness of individual experience. We die alone. In fact, we live alone. Most well-bodied people avoid that basic truth. Experience of severe illness usually allows a person to put a higher value on humanity. That seems to me a real accomplishment."

"So if this supposed wisdom only comes to those who have been ill, how is it that you know it?"

"I'm not just a psychiatrist, you know. I'm a person too. I face death and isolation just like you. You just know it better than I do. I know it from theory and from listening to others. You've done it."

"So who the hell cares?" I retorted, my voice rising.

He wavered. "I think I mentioned to you that I had a young patient with cancer." The Wizard drew a breath. "He died last week."

I watched his eyes fill with tears and felt ashamed of my persistent defensiveness. "I'm sorry."

"I think, I'm s-sure," the Wizard stammered to me across the empty bowls, "I learned more from him than I was able to give to him. I really was just there to walk him through the experience."

I pictured my father, the recalled image filtered through a video screen: the last year of his life, a Yankees baseball cap covering his moulting head, a green tartan wool bathrobe wrapping his exhausted body, his eyes defiantly bright, he spoke to the camera in small words. Later the tapes were used to train palliative care nurses. No longer restricted by his formal roles as teacher and preacher he became expressive, intimate and questioning. My father had been dour silent for most of my adolescence. On the video screen he danced and mugged, a urinary catheter swinging beneath his robe. He talked about his life, his love for my mother, us kids, and what it felt like to be close to death. In the last tape of the series he said he wanted to die. He was tired.

"My dad became much better, a more open, caring person, when he knew he was terminal. He managed to make his death into quite a triumph. He gained a lot of respect in my eyes. Before he died he showed me how to turn the pain around and use it for a greater benefit, for giving rather than for self-absorption and brooding." I spoke as gently as I could as I studied the Wizard's hazel eyes.

"Yeah, I remember," said the Wizard.

"But I want more. I want to be more than nice. I owe something for being allowed to live."

"So get what you want."

"How?"

"Going back to school is a start." He looked at his watch. "Sorry, we've got to go. I've got another patient."

Poising his left hand as if it held a pen over his lifted and flattened right, the Wizard signalled the waiter for the bill.

As he slapped his plastic card onto the tray the waiter presented, I watched a solitary woman in a blue business suit across the restaurant, near the window. She raised a teacup to her mouth.

I dropped my eyes and felt the edge of plate still warm in front of me. "Can I see you again, next week?"

"Of course," said the Wizard as he turned to the waiter and reached for the tally and the Cross pen. In large and rapid strokes his hand moved the black and silver pen in the scribble that was his signature. The paper made a tiny whooshing sound, then a crack as he snapped the carbon from the credit card tab.

"How was it?" The dark-haired waiter directed his question to me with his eyes.

I aimed my eyes at the Wizard. "Wonderful."

He smiled. "Can I give you a lift to the subway?"

Mark Coleman, M.D., F.R.C.S.(C)
R.S.MacDonald, M.D., F.R.C.S. (C)

General and Colorectal Surgery

Toronto Memorial Hospital
200 Francis Street
Toronto, Ontario

June 27,1989

Dr. Bander
242851 Wilmington Medical Center
Toronto, Ontario

Dear Dr. Bander

RE: CARR, Robin

I saw Robin in the office today. As you know she was recently in our hospital in September where I was going to revise her stoma, but found at the time that she had a thickened edematous Crohn's-like bowel and I had to do a laparotomy and a small bowel resection on September 14th. She recovered well from that operation and was discharged in six days, and our pathologist has not committed himself as to whether this is Crohn's disease or not, but I am quite certain that it is.

Because of this I think she needs to be followed by a gastroenterologist. She has moved away from Jeff Axon's area and wishes to now change and have a gastroenterologist here at the Toronto Memorial Hospital and I am going to arrange for her to have this.

Today she looks and feels quite well although she is somewhat tired because of her recent surgery. I told her I would like to see her in a couple months time before referring her on to one of our gastroenterologists.

Best Regards,

Yours Sincerely,

M.Coleman, M.D., F.R.C.S.(C)
c.c: Dr. J.Axon

Summer

The veranda door banged. Parker leapt upon my bed and hurried his compact, soft, black body to a warm spot in the blankets. He snuggled into me looking for protection. The kids screamed through the door in pursuit. Jean and Jamie halted at the end of my bed and giggled.

"Parker, come here. Here Parker. Here little doggie," they called in stage whispers.

My mother's black cocker spaniel didn't budge. Parker had found his refuge.

Gordon came to the porch door.

"Leave Parker alone. Aunt Robin is trying to sleep." I kept my eyes closed until the door clicked shut.

The air held the moist chill of an early summer morning in the Eastern Townships of Quebec. It smelt musky on the veranda. Taking a second deep breath, I smelled the cool water of Brome Lake.

Our old, roughly built cottage sloped from decades of heavy snow. Peach floral curtains faded in one window; beige textured cloth draped another. Agreeably, the whole house remained dishevelled and mismatched. I slept on the lopsided back porch. The house was full. Only the bathroom and the kitchen held no beds. In one bedroom my older brother and sister-in-law slept in a double bed end-to-end with the kids' two cots. An aunt, uncle and cousin slept in the living room on a pull-out couch and an air-mattress. Mom, who lived here all summer, had her own room. My younger brother slept on the front porch. Parker slept wherever he could find a spot.

I rose from the old iron bed.

"Sorry, Parker."

He jumped off the bed and watched me dress.

"Okay," I said as I opened the porch door that led to the kitchen, "you're on your own."

I headed for the coffee in the kitchen. The little black spaniel shadowed me. Over the chirping of birds I heard kids' squeals from the lawn by the lake. I glanced at the clock: 5:45 a.m. Opening the cupboard door, I surveyed the collection of cups: clan tartans, out-of-style patterns, souvenirs from Nova Scotia, the last survivor of my grandmother's set, joke gifts, and an ugly pottery mug my father used to keep at his office. I had made it at Sunday school when I was twelve. Its mouth was deliberately oversized to allow my father's large nose entry to the bowl. Despite the mug's roughness, my father had seemed delighted by my consideration for his worst feature.

I made a large pot of coffee, poured the mug full and from the uneven thick rim drank in the warm comfort of the caffeine. There must be an adult out there with the kids, I thought. I took an ironstone mug with a playing card pattern on it and filled it with coffee and milk.

Hushed, Parker and I walked past our sleeping relatives to the front door of the cottage. The racket of children increased as I opened the outside door. My older brother sat slumped in a chair on the deck, his feet resting on the railing. His angular thin face was unshaven, his eyes unwashed of sleep. One side of the collar of his red golf shirt bent up. He wore navy blue rugger shorts. He had worn variations of this uniform for ten years.

Silently I handed him the coffee. He nodded and I dropped into the chair beside him. Parker hid behind my feet.

We sipped our coffee, blowing on its surface to make the steam rise and said nothing. Gordon and I sat awed by the legacy of the lake. Our mother's family was large and Anglo-Quebecoise. Fearing Quebec's separation from Canada, economic decline, and pro-francophone legislation, all but two of our six uncles had fled Quebec in the seventies. But the family cottages remained and the annual pilgrimage persisted. Gordon and his family camped along their way from Spring Grove, Alberta. Aunt Beth and Uncle Dan flew in from Edmonton. Cousins drove in from Montreal, Bayfield, Sarnia, Oakville, London, Toronto, Cobourg, Labrador and Prince Rupert. This summer we gathered for the wedding of the youngest cousin.

Our family had been on this lake for sixty years. The fourth generation romped on the lawn in front of us.

Most of my childhood summers had been spent at Brome Lake. I learned to swim in the lake. My mother grew up spending winters in Montreal, summers here. Five years ago, after my father's death, I brought my mother to the original house, on the other side of the lake. For several hours a day, she sat staring at the water, saying nothing. The lake gave her some peace. Now I returned to Brome to recuperate from my ninth surgery and to attend a family wedding.

Fog lay heavy on the broad, gleaming surface of the lake. Above the water line in the distance peaked roofs capping tar-paper shacks and mansions. United Empire Loyalists, like my mother's family, the Humphreys, had made homesteads in this part of Quebec. Now the Eastern Townships, Les Cantons de l'Est, were mixed French and English. Hyundai produced cars here. Americans skied. From the deck, the ski runs carved into mountains that surrounded the lake were easily viewed. As a child, I had considered them immense. Now that my elder brother lived by the Rockies, they became Beginner's Hills. To the left cut Bolton Pass, an access road through the mountains. Each Thanksgiving, my father and I had driven through, awed by the splendid colours. He had believed in God as nature.

I sat in silence by my brother and knew I belonged here, maybe not forever but for a while.

Jean and Jamie tumbled and wrestled and shouted. They were five and three years old respectively, and they knew just where my brother's limits of tolerance lay. Mine were being tested.

"More coffee, Robbie?"

I handed Gordon my mug. No one else called me Robbie.

He went into the cottage. I went down to the dock, closer to the lake.

Jamie saw my movement as an invitation to tackle. His little lightweight body clung to my leg and he growled.

"Oh a lion, eh?" I picked him up and flung him over my shoulder. "Well, I know lions don't like to get wet!" I swung him into my arms and cradled him over the water. He squealed in delight.

Jean flew down the steps.

"Don't worry, Jamie, I'll save you." She grabbed my

leg. "Okay you monster, let go of my brother!" Jean ordered.

I roared and sank to the dock to maintain my balance. The three of us rolled together.

Parker stood at the top of the concrete stairs wagging his stump of a tail at us, the white spot on his throat — considered an allowable flaw in his otherwise perfect jet coat — exposed.

"Careful. Careful now." A crag just beneath the surface, lay below the dock's brink, to the left. To the other side a boat's cradle threatened with keen edges and studded joints. "Quick, quick, let's hide under the canoe before your dad comes back."

The ancient battered canoe lay upside down on the grass, a safe distance from the water. My niece and nephew bounded for the hiding place. I crawled under the canoe with them. The smell of baby powder and Jamie's diaper filled the enclosed damp space beneath the hull.

"Shh, or your dad will hear us."

Jean studied me for a long moment.

"Your dad is dead."

"That's right."

"You're my daddy's sister."

"That's right. I'm your aunt. My father died the day you were born."

The cottage door slammed. The kids giggled.

"Oh where, oh where could they be?" Gordon said loudly from the stairs.

A short silence as Gordon crossed the lawn, then thump, thud, thump, thump, bang, above our heads on the canoe's hull. Jamie and Jean squealed and sprang to attack Gordon.

"I'm a tiger," yelled Jean, clinching Gordon's thigh.

"And I'm a lion," roared Jamie as he grappled with his father's shin.

Gordon calculated his fall to the dew-glazed grass and yelled, "You got me. You got me."

"Lions and Tigers, and Bears, oh my!" I whispered to the three bodies rolling patterns in the dew.

Gordon's children wriggled, wet under each of his arms.

I pulled Jamie off the wrangle of bodies and kissed his smooth cheek before setting him on his unsure feet. He waddled, in his plump diaper, up the lawn. His chubby arm flung up with each stride. "You can't get me. You can't get me," he called.

Parker followed at a distance.

My brother lifted Jean over his chest then swung her down by his side. She screamed as he tickled her mercilessly.

"Shh, the whole house will be up," I said to Gordon.

He shrugged his shoulders, his laughter ringing.

Some people never change, I thought.

Mom, my younger brother Alan, and Gordon's spouse Susan appeared on the deck, mugs in hands. Parker greeted them. I joined them and let Gordon proceed with the wrestling match. Alan gave me his chair and his coffee and descended to help the kids beat on Gordon. Uncle Mike, Aunt Amy and my cousin Francis emerged from the damp cottage. They all sat blowing on their coffee, stunned by the early morning sunlight.

"I'm going to North Hatley to go to church," I said to my mother.

"You?" My mother appeared surprised, but pleased.

"Well, it's a pretty drive."

"You know your father used to preach at that church."

"No kidding," I said pretending not to know.

I noticed everyone sat listening. As if a sip might distort her hearing, Susan sat immobile, eyes down, mouth pursed above but not drawing coffee from her mug. My cousin Francis watched my mother and me directly. A little smirk twisted her mouth. Uncle Mike and Aunt Amy pretended to watch the kids.

"Anyone want to come?" I said looking around at their sleepy faces. I hoped they wouldn't.

No one answered. Francis shifted her attention to my brothers' game on the lawn.

I went to the cottage and changed from my jeans into a dress my mother made for me the previous year.

Car keys jingling beneath her fingers, my mother said, "Take mine."

"Thanks," I said as I closed the last button at the nape of my neck.

My mother surveyed my chest. "Don't you ever wear a bra?"

I lifted one eyebrow and glared at her. Not this again. We've been doing this for sixteen years.

She made a gesture: lifting a hand, averting her eyes, turning her head to the left, then nimbly flicking her hand. It was family code for 'sorry I spoke'. I recognized the signal as a legacy from my mother's mother.

She left the room without another word.

I got in my mother's car and pulled onto the dirt road that lead to the autoroute.

So Dad, where are you?

The road to North Hatley twisted between mountains, huddled along ledges that dropped abruptly to lakes. It wound through farms and connected villages. It flattened where glaciers had pulled back centuries ago, and spilled water over massive expanses. A final turn and plunge down the mountain, and North Hatley appeared suddenly, quietly by Lake Massawippi. North Hatley was built by Confederates searching to vacation north of Yankee territory. The architecture remained an odd mix of Atlanta plantation and New England clapboard. Lake Massawippi ran a deep gaunt line pinched between mountains, but it was the Unitarian church I sought.

I followed the road to the end of the lake. The white-washed wood frame church perched on the slope just as it had since 1847, spared of exterior decoration, a squat boxy design supported a simple squared steeple. My heart started to pound as I parked the car. The last time I had attended church was my father's funeral, this date, five years earlier.

After crossing the threshold and adjusting my eyes, I saw the bare interior of the church. Pews spanned the length of the building, only four rows deep, before a pulpit to the side. Garden flowers stood in a pottery vase. Slates of dark wood, perhaps oak, covered the walls, meeting each other in herringbone joints. No crosses. No saints. No promise of salvation. The only stained glass, a meek arrangement of multi-hued squares stood behind the lectern. At the lake end of the church, clear vintage glass rippled in its wooden frame.

I looked for signs of my father but saw none.

Tinkles of piano keys filled the church and I sat down in a pew. I squinted toward the music and found an adolescent with hair shaved to bristles on one side, falling to collar-length curls on the other. A high-pitched buzz came from the back of the church and I turned to find the source, an aged man with a cane, a white tennis shirt and a hearing aid. Everyone seemed to know him.

Black academic robes covered the young minister. A sash embroidered with folk art images of flowers and birds hung around his thick neck. His brilliant red hair and beard sprung from his head at strange angles. He stroked his red bristles nervously.

"Let us welcome the unseen spirits of Faith, Hope and Love," he said opening his arms to the congregation.

Christ, here we go, I thought.

At the back of the congregation a woman stood. About fifty, with scrubbed fair skin, her gray hair pulled back to a long braid. Her build was hidden beneath a loose, unornamented, blue dress. Ugly, functional leather sandals covered her feet. Any sensuality she possessed she disguised well.

I bet she's the local Girl Guide leader. I'll call her Brown Owl.

With her hands folded in front, Brown Owl cleared her throat and spoke in a monotone:

"On behalf of the congregation, I would like to welcome you, Reverend Beamish, your wife Amanda, and of course, little Aaron. We hope that you will enjoy your stay with us this summer and that we will learn and grow together."

Brown Owl sat. The young Reverend Beamish nodded his blazing red head and began again.

In the back pew the buzz of the hearing aid grew to a whistle. The reverend moved closer to the front row and strained to speak louder without shouting.

I'll call him The Newly Ordained Reverend of Zeal.

He talked to the children about a greasy chicken shack — Harold's — in a rough section of Chicago. He expounded about the smell of the chicken on the wind, and how anticipating its taste made the hazard of the trip worthwhile.

I should have gone swimming.

Waves of light reflected off the lake water and shimmied on the ceiling panels. I shifted in discomfort on the hard wooden bench and anticipated the end of the sermon.

"Adventure. What you should remember is that anticipation, dreaming, regardless of failure or the possibility of failure, is a large part of the joy of life. Failure is not such a big deal if you learn to enjoy the anticipation and excitement of trying. And the joy of life is something worthy of trying."

He smiled at the children and returned to his place behind the lectern.

What did I anticipate? Getting ill again. Chronic disease had cheated me out of many summers. Five summers in a row, I had spent weeks in the abattoir. Always bracketing surgery was denial of illness, then recovery from the invasion. Several years before the surgeries began, when the disease first grew in me, illness had stunted my summers with fevers, skin and eye infections, blunt pain, rectal bleeding and exhaustion. I wanted to reclaim what illness had stolen from me, to seize summer bare-chested and squeeze it. I wanted to hug every gasp of life from it and take its breath as my own.

The Reverend's voice interrupted my thoughts. I glanced at my watch. July eighth. My father died July fifth. I saw Reverend Zeal's eyes catch my movement. I stiffened. He smiled.

"Up until now I was too willing to see the heat of

summer as a nuisance. I was too willing to rush into the air-conditioning and make the year's weather homogenous. I was too willing to see summer as a passing phenomenon of little consequence."

He paused to let his words sink into the congregation. I sank, bored, into the bench.

Reverend Zeal faced the congregation. As if the thought had just occurred to him, he fumbled through several paperback books. He began to read aloud, "Three poor boys hauled manure in the intense heat of summer." Surprised by his choice of images, I closed my eyes and let them impress me.

"Flies and stench rose off the wheel barrows as they laboured. At the end of that long day the three boys rested, exhausted on a fence. From the marsh they heard the frogs singing their joy. What was there to be joyous about? Life was not so good.

"One of the boys picked up a corn husk and began to saw out a tune to the chorus of frogs. The other boys swung as partners."

I imagined myself with them in the dust, dancing.

I opened my eyes and saw the final flip of the Reverend Zeal's jig. His black robes settled around him, but amusement remained on his red bristled face. I smiled.

"What I would like to encourage you to do is to embrace summer. I would like us all to welcome summer and find joy in it. Notice summer. Pay attention to it. Christianity has forgotten the joy of life. Does one have to die to find joy? Surely as Unitarians, we would all find that difficult to believe. But as Unitarians, we also are likely to think of the pursuit of joy as trivial. We think joy is not serious enough to warrant our full attention and we would be shallow people to pursue it. But surely joy is the responsibility of all humanity to find where and how it can. Many of us think we are unworthy of joy."

My heart pulsed in my throat. I raised my hand to cover my mouth. Do I think I am unworthy? Or do I think joy is beyond my grasp? Was I being punished by disease? For what? I expect life to be a struggle. I had come to think of happiness as banal, even boring, something reserved for less complicated lives, ones that required less fight. But I don't believe in destiny. Dad raised me as a Unitarian. I don't believe in the hand of God, a grand plan, or sin and punishment. I believe it's up to me. Just me and only me. Don't I?

I heard the Reverend Zeal's voice: "We are not unworthy of joy. Nor is the search for joy a trivial pursuit. Joy can be made and joy can be found. Anticipate life and its adventures regardless of its failures. Enjoy it. Taste summer. Embrace summer. I ask you to allow summer into your heart."

He descended the pulpit and walked down the middle aisle to the door. The pianist began a Beatles' tune. The congregation stood to leave. I sat alone and wondered what to do.

At the open door of the church came a clatter as the ancient man with the hearing aid greeted the young Reverend Zeal.

"So glad to meet you. So happy you're here with us. Loved your lecture. I didn't catch it all, of course, but I'm so glad you're here."

The minister laughed and the two men briskly shook hands. I stood and moved toward the door.

"Do you have any notes that could help me?" continued the old man.

"You wouldn't be able to read my writing," said the Reverend Zeal.

"Eh?"

"NO," yelled the minister still trapped in a handshake, searching for an escape. I stepped forward and offered my right hand. Our eyes met. I winked. He twinkled.

"Thank you," he said taking my hand.

"No. Thank you," I said.

He moved to the next parishioner. I moved into the church hall for tea.

Brown Owl approached me with her sense of duty. I spoke first.

"I noticed your church is arranged lengthwise. Is that usual for Unitarian churches of the time?"

"No," she said. "The pulpit used to be at the far end, in front of the window, overlooking the lake. A minister we had years back had it moved to the side and the pews rowed lengthwise so he wouldn't have to compete with the view."

I laughed. That's my Dad.

Brown Owl directed me to a white-clothed table laid with four Brown Betty teapots and an assortment of china cups and saucers.

She touched each pot's lid as she spoke, "Camomile, Earl Gray, Coffee, Decaf."

"Earl Gray, please."

"Milk?"

Her pouring of the tea was expert: milk first, then tea. Not a drop more than needed fell from the spout. I had forgotten the tradition. In characterless styrofoam cups or tepid in hospital plastic, tea became a different drink. This tea, tea sipped in a church hall out of a bone china cup, was a relic of a time not devoted to convenience. The proper service of tea took time and manners. I drank from a yellow teacup as I had been taught by my grandmother. Beneath the cup I supported the saucer with my left hand, my right pinky finger extended as I lifted the fine china rim to my lips. The comfort of custom. The satisfaction of knowing what it is you are supposed to do. How strange to belong so easily.

Members of the congregation chatted to tourists and children ran around anxious to get on with the summer day.

I crossed the church to gaze out the old rippled glass window to the lake. Watching the surface of Lake Massawippi sparkle in the morning light, I remembered my last conversation with my father. We were both in hospitals, he in Ottawa, I in Toronto. Heavy doses of morphine filled both of us.

Over the phone he said, "Can you feel my hands in yours?"

"Yes, Dad,"

"We'll go hand in hand over the waves of the St. Lawrence," he said, and I knew he would soon be dead. It was voluntary euthanasia. He told my mother to allow no further medical intervention and he let go of his life.

Lake Massawippi continued its never-ending-dance. The old pane seemed more fluid under its reflected light.

Yes, this view might intimidate a preacher, even Dad. I shifted my eyes and focused on the wood of the window. Summer, I thought. I continued to stare at the window, turning the warm teacup in my hands. Detecting motion I peered through the glass. The punk-haired pianist hurried, sheet music tucked under his arm, down the road toward the lake.

Probably going swimming. That's what I should do too.

I returned the teacup and headed for the car.

Driving back to Brome Lake, the sky arced high and untouchable, its blue, burning. The wind stirred cumulus clouds. I opened my eyes wide in the cool shadows, squinting against the blaring sunlight when the clouds passed off the highway.

Sweat collected in the crease of my knee, then dribbled down my calf. It was summer indeed.

I took the Lac Brome cut-off, passed my mother's road on Rock Island Bay, and continued past Robinson Bay and Cedar Bay to Bondville Road. Making the turn to the original house, now owned by my youngest uncle, I parked my mother's car at the top of the hill and walked down the patched cement trail to the lake.

As a child, I had spent every summer here with an assortment of my twenty-one cousins, twelve aunts and uncles, grandparents and brothers. My grandfather Humphrey, a poor man with seven children, had bought lake frontage during the Depression. They were one of the lucky families. Granddad worked for Canada Cement his whole life, without lay-offs. When money became available, rooms were added, one at a time, to the original two-room structure. Granddad and my uncles learned carpentry as they went. Each of the seven families had a single room. Bunk beds and iron framed beds flanked one another. Built of scrap lumber on shallow concrete foundations of uneven quality, the floor pitched and tossed from room to room. Not a single door fit its frame. The roof buckled and bowed and threatened to collapse every winter. The family joked that moss held the roof together.

Granddad erected a cement and stone wall to hold back the earth from the water. With a nail we all scratched our initials in the concrete. Being the children of the only daughter, my brothers and I had unique letters. Every winter the wall collapsed under the grind of lake ice. Every spring Granddad made a new one. He loved to construct things with children. I often wondered if he mixed the cement wrong just so he could keep doing it.

Every year Granddad put a bird house in the towering blue spruce by the shore. It was built of leftover wood and coated with the same dark green that he painted everything he made. We came to call the colour Lucky's Green after one of the dogs, a wire-haired terrier called Lucky, got into it and trailed green throughout the house. Long after Granddad died, the swallows returned to the lucky green bird house. As I stood there watching, two swooped, chasing each other across the lake's surface. A sudden upturn and the duet was broken.

Lawns never survived in front of the original house. Twenty-four grandchildren had trampled the ground smooth playing Kick the Can, Ghost in the Graveyard, Scrub and wrestling with many dogs. Standing on the new growth of grass I realized that I had never before been alone at this house.

Wonder where everybody is. A dog should have come out to see me by now.

I knew the house would be unlocked. The back door didn't even keep the flies out, but I climbed the hill and drove back towards my mother's place.

Cars marked by a variety of provincial license plates stood parked in the lane outside my mother's lucky green house. I parked hers and walked toward the cottage. Three dogs trotted up to greet me: Parker, Hero, my uncle's big blond lab, and a huge bear-like, black and white Newfie puppy I'd never seen before. I squatted to let them lick the salt from my sweaty skin. Hero's gait seemed pained. Hip dysplasia. I stroked back his golden ears.

"Ain't no justice to it, Hero."

Hero weighed a mere twenty pounds less than I, but his bulk condensed to a smaller muscular body, propelled by four webbed paws. Despite his unsure hindquarters Hero could easily knock me over, but he never did. Now he flipped his tongue around my wrist. His mouth felt soft. Playfully he gnawed on my bone without breaking the skin. My wrist reddened.

"Okay, that's enough." I pulled my arm away and kissed his wide skull between his eyes.

I looked at the massive puppy. Its tongue hung dripping from a smiling mouth. I ran my hands through the dense black and white fur.

"You must be hotter than hell."

The pup tumbled to the ground without control and rolled to expose its belly to me. Obediently, I rubbed.

"You are a goof, aren't ya."

Parker nuzzled my wrist.

"Jealous?"

I took the black spaniel's feathered silky ears and tied them to a loose knot over his domed head. My father gave Parker to my mother a year before he died. I pictured my father in his hospital bed in the dining room, Parker curled up by his side, watching basketball on tv, his hand stroking Parker.

"Hey Park, where's Mom?" I said looking into his

dark eyes. Parker tossed his head and knocked his ears back to place.

I found her in the kitchen with Aunt Benta, chatting, opening beers, making lemonade and searching for napkins all at once. Mom loves company. My mother and I are very different.

As usual, Mom wore pink. She's a short, cute, gray-haired lady whose frame has thickened with the years. Her demeanour is doggedly cheerful, steadfast in its sanity, and blessedly uncomplicated. The neighbourhood kids still call her "Cuddles."

The last few months of my father's life, my mother had coffee with him every morning in the hospital. She cooked his favourite dinners, took it to the hospital and ate with my father every night.

A year after my father died Mom phoned and said she had problems sleeping.

"I understand," I said, "after thirty-five years of sleeping with Dad, you miss him."

"No, I mean, I've never been alone." Her voice cracked. "I slept in the same bed as my grandmother until the day I got married. When your father travelled, one of you kids used to sleep with me. Don't you remember?"

Mom was baffled when my marriage failed, enraged when my surgery failed and heartbroken when my father died. The thought of her inevitable death terrified me more than my own.

I crossed the kitchen and kissed my mother. "Why didn't you remind me this morning they were all going to be here?"

"Why?" Mom said.

"I could have helped. I didn't have to go to North Hatley."

She laughed. "I know better than to try and change your mind once you've decided to do something, especially if it's something you want to do alone."

She handed me a tray lined with beer bottles and glasses. "Pass these around, will you?"

"Is the Road to Hell here?"

"Don't call your Aunt Ingrid that!" Mom scolded me.

"How did you know it was Ingrid I was talking about?"

Mom grinned. "Just stay out of her way Robin."

At the front of the cottage, I took a deep breath and opened the door. Strewn across the deck, the lawn and the lake were more than forty of my family, all sizes, shapes, ages, hair colours, temperaments and beliefs. My cousin Ray, twenty-three, stout, dark and self-effacing, played with Hero. A cluster of other cousins watched. My second eldest uncle, Stephen, a blond cowboy, complete with tooled boots sat on the lawn debating with a couple of his younger brothers. Aunt Janine, a chic, auburn-haired French woman of independent character and quick tongue, held court on the deck with a group of female relatives clad in shorts and sun dresses.

"Well, well, look who finally decided to show up," came Uncle Mark's voice from one corner of the deck. A man in his early fifties, he was my grandparents' sixth child.

"Let someone else do that Robin; there's no need to tire yourself," cut the Road to Hell's shrill voice from another corner. She and Mark shared an uneasy marriage.

Thirty-five years ago, she trained as a nurse in Montreal.

For five years she worked at the Royal Vic. She thought her obsolete medical knowledge exceeded my daily experience with my body. She saw me as an illustration of the proverb: There but for the grace of God go I. I loathed her pity.

"Hair of the dog," Uncle Rob's best friend, Larry, a local sporting a John Deere tractor cap, beckoned me to his corner of the deck.

I used the tray to pass from one person to another without stopping for conversation. With the empty tray, I ran back to the kitchen.

Let me out of here, I thought.

Mom recognized the panic on my face. "Go swimming if you don't want to talk to them."

I hugged her. "You know me too well."

"No kidding," Mom said picking up a tray loaded with full bottles and empty glasses. "Back in a minute, Benta," she called on her way out.

In the bathroom I changed into a black and green one-piece bathing suit. I fussed with my ileostomy, adjusting it then checking the mirror to confirm its camouflage.

I paused at the cottage door, looked down and examined my abdomen again, then straightened my shoulders and opened the door.

As I crossed the deck I caught the Road to Hell's gaze scrutinizing my abdomen. In my mind I pointed to the right of my navel and said: Here. It's right here. Can't tell, can you.

She shifted her stare and I continued down to the lake.

Jean and Alan sputtered and kicked in the water. Alan is stocky, blond and freckle-faced. His features are broad, not angular. He looks so unlike Gordon or me, that we used to tell him our parents bought him at the Salvation Army for a quarter. He believed us.

Gordon and Susan sat in deck chairs watching their offspring.

Holding a stick I called the dogs. I pitched the stick off the dock and the three dogs scrambled after it. Parker, the eldest, smallest and most docile of the three, made no effort to compete. His ears floated out behind him as he paddled in a small circle beyond the dock and headed for shore.

"Some working dog you are, Parker," called Alan.

"More like a cushion," Susan laughed.

Parker hauled himself up on the dock, positioned himself in front of the deck chairs and shook away his wetness, soaking his critics. Satisfied, Parker trotted up the stairs.

Hero won the stick. His noble, golden head high in the water, Hero made for shore. The oversized puppy trailed him.

Alan and I splashed each other. The kids joined in. The dogs barked and leapt trying to bite the water as it separated in the air. Jamie, his hair slicked to his skull, his Canadiens hockey jersey darkened and dripping with water, chased Parker back up the stairs.

The Road came down to the dock to watch our play.

I dove in the water and surfaced several feet out from the dock. I pushed hair back from my face.

"You can still swim?"

"Of course, I can still swim, and I can still swim better than most," I shot back to her.

"But you and your father..." She hesitated. I glared at her. Come on you coward, say it. Tell me I should lie still and conserve my energy like a nice young consumptive lady.

"Well, your father always looked like a whale in the water," she continued.

My brothers stiffened.

"Dad was fat. I'm not. Besides whales swim pretty damned good." I pushed at the water with my feet.

You buried my father long before he died too, I thought.

"I want to come with you. Dad says you're the best swimmer," called Jean as I turned away and began to swim the crawl. Everyday, before I got ill, I swam a mile in thirty-five minutes. My right arm in the water brushed my side. My left extended forward in the air, then cut the lake's surface without a splash and pulled back. I turned my head slightly out of the water, inhaled through my nostrils, then turning my face toward the lake bottom blew bubbles from my mouth. My arms rotated in large synchronized circles. My legs kicked at the cool water. My body stretched long in the water.

The rhythm began to build. Each time I raised my face to take in air I saw the mountain at the end of the lake. Water, air, mountain, arm, water, air, mountain, arm. My muscles warmed against the cool water, and air swelled my lungs. I felt joy behind my nose. From its confined hiding place in my head, it expanded, moving down my body finding the voids, filling long-ignored hollows. Water, air, mountain, arm, water, air, mountain, arm, joy. Joy, as I lifted my face higher from the water to see the clouds over the mountains. Joy, as my abdomen muscles pulled taut with every kick. I felt joy in my toes, so far away. My body moved in mechanical metre, leaving my mind free to watch. I tasted the water. I felt the weeds brush me. I anticipated every breath. By the changing perspective of the mountain I judged the distance I had crossed. I listened and noted the sound of children far away. I heard a boat's motor. I raised my head to use both eyes to judge its position safely distant.

My rhythm broken and my arms tired, I turned and side-stroked toward the dock, still watching the clouds on the mountain.

I flipped to my belly and began the breast stroke. Submerging my head during the glide, I sought air after every rotation. Elongation of the body, then contraction. In the air, water ran from my brow and into my eyes. I blinked and saw the fuzzy image of the Road standing on the dock. I saw Jean and Jamie and wondered if either of them would host disease. A twist of my shoulder and I floated on my back, part of the big surface of Brome Lake. I glanced at my wrist and saw a bruise forming from the pinch of Hero's teeth. Drifting and hearing myself breathe, I touched my head, my heart and my ileostomy. I've got all this, I thought.

Lungs filled, back arched, eyes closed, I pushed my feet down and sank suspended below the surface, letting oxygen bubble from my mouth until I was empty. I counted the seconds, waiting on instinct. One kick and I broke the surface. My mouth opened and sucked at the air.

I smiled alone in the water.

Toronto Memorial Hospital
Department of Radiology

Name:	CARR, Robin	**Date of Procedure**:	13/09/90
MRN:	090 01 10	**Date Dictated:**	13/09/90
Location:	OP	**Date Printed:**	19/09/90
			09:47

Physician: Mark Coleman MD

Procedures Performed: Colon, without air contrast

ILEOSTOMY INJECTION

A Foley catheter was inserted into the ileostomy site and barium was run retrograde. There was opacification of the small bowel to the level of the mid-jejunum.

The distal segment of small bowel terminating at the ileostomy site appears diseased with narrowing of the lumen, ulceration and pseudo sacculation. The proximal length of the diseased segment is 10 to 20 cm.

The barium emptied into the ileostomy bag at the end of the procedure indicating that there is not a total obstruction.

Read by Paul Stern   Reviewed by Iain Roberts

Other Side of the Curtain

She pressed an I.V. needle against my forearm. I had dehydrated and become blind but I recognized the needle's enormous gauge as it punctured my skin. They were preparing me for surgery. My veins sank deeper into my flesh. The target vein rolled and the I.V. missed.

"You've had a lot of these?"

"I had my tenth surgery six days ago," I said flatly.

"It shows. You're veins are scarred. Again," she said and again she missed. The nurse plunged the needle into my right hand on the third attempt. After several twists of the needle and adjustments to the angle of entry, my blood flowed back through the needle. I felt the nurse connect a long plastic tube and saline washed into my dry tissue.

Minutes later my sight returned. First, swelling dots of light, then black spots softly collapsing. I saw the senior nurse. She was in her mid-fifties, mouth untouched by lipstick, nails trimmed short and scrubbed. A starched, pressed, perfectly-fitted white uniform covered her husky frame. Her hair, dyed to a flat brown, curled stiffly into order. As neat and correct as a military officer, she slipped my arms through a hospital gown, noted my temperature, my blood pressure and disappeared through the drawn beige curtain without a word.

From the other side of the curtain I heard another

patient arrive in emergency on an ambulance stretcher. Her thin, high voice sounded young, eighteen, perhaps twenty. A young male doctor began the initial interview with her. I closed my eyes and listened.

"So what seems to be the problem?" His voice nudged toward cheerful.

"Well, I'm bleeding," said the young woman.

"Bleeding? Where?"

I heard the sheets rustle as she gestured.

"You mean you've got your period? So what?" laughed the young doctor.

"It's been two weeks."

"Have you been to see a gynaecologist?"

"A what?" She snapped her chewing gum.

"So, I'll take your history," he said and left to get the necessary papers. I heard her sigh and fidget behind the curtain.

I shifted and pulled the sheets around me. I found my glasses in my purse and put them on to watch the I.V. drip.

The doctor returned and asked her name, age and weight. I didn't hear the replies.

"A little light aren't you?"

The woman peeped in response.

"What do you do? Are you a student?"

"I work in a club," I heard her say.

"Oh yeah, what do you do there?" His interest sounded genuine.

"I dance."

The doctor paused two beats then said, "You mean you strip."

"Yeah."

In the corridor the intercom called, and more patients

were wheeled by on stretchers. Pain boiled in my gut, but I strained to ignore it. I concentrated on my ears.

"Are you involved in any prostitution?"

"No." Her tone stayed even.

"Do you expect me to believe that?"

"Why not?" she said. "What do you know about it?"

"Any history of sexually-transmitted diseases?" His voice reverted to distracted professionalism.

"No."

The silence sharpened. I tried to imagine the expressions on their faces.

"Do you know what sexually-transmitted disease is?"

"Yeah," she said.

"I'll get a nurse. I'm going to do a pelvic examination."

As he left the room the curtain bellowed out behind him. The young woman cursed quietly to herself.

I noticed stains on my side of the curtain, brown spatters of dried liquid. Blood spots? I looked up at the ceiling. The trail continued up there. I shivered at the possible explanations.

The doctor returned with the senior nurse. She parted the curtain. "Someone is coming down from the ninth floor to see you." She thrust a stainless steel basin at me then closed the curtain without waiting for a response.

They didn't explain anything to the young woman.

"Spread your legs," the doctor said.

I heard the clicking of a machine.

"Ouch. Ow. Ow. OW!" She began to weep.

I put one hand on my forehead and one on my abdomen. I pulled my knees up and pressed them close together. My left hand moved from my forehead to cover my mouth. I let the air out of my nose in a long hiss.

The young dancer cried.

"Don't be silly," came the sharp voice of the nurse.

I retched. Embarrassed by the deep croaking noise, I forgot about the basin and hauled myself up on the bed's side-rail and vomited. I heard them finish the examination and leave the high-pitched young voice sobbing and whimpering. A black orderly in a white uniform cleaned the puddle I had made on the floor.

I said, "I'm sorry," to the curtain as the clinical clerk came in. A pretty boy with blond curls, gold chains and rings, and a million-dollar smirk, I figured his father was a dentist. Five days ago he had been unable to draw a blood sample out of my arm and had to pull blood from a larger vein in my groin. His hands trembled when he took it.

"Didn't you just get out?" asked the clinical clerk.

"Friday," I said. This was Sunday morning.

"I see they have the I.V. started." He fingered the plastic tubing while he studied the board of gadgets behind the bed's headboard. His sleeve grazed my cheek as he reached over me for the blood pressure cuff. He fumbled with the velcro opening, then circled my arm with the cuff. Twice he gauged my blood pressure lying down then sitting up. It surprised me he knew how to read it.

"What do you think it is?"

"I'm obstructed," I said. "I ate an orange."

"How many times have you vomited?"

I hesitated. "Ten."

He looked at me and I knew he knew I lied. I had

vomited seventeen times, waiting until 5 a.m to call Lucy for help.

"I think you're obstructed. I'm going to put down a nasogastric tube."

"No," I said, keeping my voice steady.

He turned and leered at me. "No? Why not?"

"I've had them before and I hate them. No thank you."

"You're throwing up too much and your abdomen is extended. You've got to have one." He turned and left through the curtain.

My intestine wrung and I vomited again, this time into the kidney-shaped pan the nurse had given me.

A fresh-faced blonde nurse returned with the novice doctor. Wheels creaked as a large low glass jar connected to suction rolled in on a gray metal trolley.

"It won't be easy," I said. "My nasal passages are very small and I hate those things." I tried not to sound hysterical but I felt my throat already tightening.

He ripped the tube from the package and started to roll it in clear gelatinous lubricant.

"Don't you have anything smaller? Some people are smaller you know." I tried to ease myself with a joke.

"No, but they DO come bigger," he said.

I fell quiet. My eyes narrowed and furrows creased my forehead.

"Right." He handed me a styrofoam coffee cup filled with tepid water and a straw. "Drink this when I tell you."

He moved to the right side of the bed. The young nurse stayed on the left.

I tried to distract myself by thinking of a name for him, but my strategy wasn't working. I panicked. Not my face. Not my head. I tried to force my feeling down to my toes, but all my energy gathered in my eyes focused on the tube in his bejewelled hand. His nails were chewed. I took my glasses off.

The clinical clerk approached me, hose in hand.

"Now, relax and swallow when I tell you." He started shoving hard clear plastic through my nostril. The tube struck the back of my sinus, refusing to turn down to my stomach. I gagged, flung up my hand and knocked his hand and the tube out of my nose. As blood seeped into my mouth I began to cry.

"No," I sobbed out loud.

"Yes," he persisted. "We'll try again."

He did, but without success. I wept uncontrollably. I hung my head and padded a gauze compress at my bleeding nostril.

"I'll be back in a minute," the doctor called over his shoulder as he pushed back the curtain in irritation.

I remembered high school science experiments with frogs and vomited again.

He returned proudly displaying a spray can.

"Local anesthetic," he said as he approached me. The blonde nurse returned to her station at my left side. I reached for her hand and squeezed it.

"All right," she said.

He pushed the nozzle in my nostril and sprayed. I choked and hacked as tingling penetrated my head.

"Swallow it. Swallow it."

I did as ordered. My eyes watered. My throat numbed.

The doctor pounced upon me, forcing in the tube. I screamed and raised my hands to slap him away, but the young nurse caught my wrists, then lowered them.

"Drink. Drink. Drink!" he yelled at me. The plastic tube descended to my swampy convulsing stomach as I drank. I retched.

"No. NO," they yelled together. The hose curled in my stomach, but it didn't rise with the vomit. They connected me to the bell jar and secured the tube with pink plastic tape to the end of my nose. With a large safety pin the nurse pierced the blue gown and attached the NG tube.

"Wouldn't want it to inadvertently fall out," she said.

I kept my eyes lowered. I vomited again around the tube. The nurse parted the curtain and left.

I followed the trail of bilge leading from my face to the jar. I.V. tubes, rectal tubes, surgical drains, urinary catheters, and ileostomies remained private, hidden beneath sheets or clothes. This tube sat displayed. The jar gathered the contents of my stomach ready for inspection by anyone. No place to hide. The tube scraped my throat with every swallow. I tried to breathe through my nose and suffocated. My spirit rose higher in my head and pressed against my skull. The only place left to go was out.

The novice doctor returned with a red-rubber hose pinched between his gnawed fingernails. "We need to insert this into your bowel."

I swiped the hose from him. "I'll do it myself. I have more experience with ostomies than you."

Don't cry. Things could be worse. There's been worse than this, much worse. I removed the bag and pressed the red-rubber slowly down through my ileostomy.

Behind the drawn curtain I sat alone and wept for three hours. I heard the cries of a woman in labour and envied her. She would get something for her pain. An old woman with angina wailed and I pitied her. I heard the intercom call the alarm for a heart attack. Someone screamed, "Murderer! Murderer!" and pounded the wall beside me as a parent died. I tried not to harden. I tried not to close down.

Lucy and the surgical fellow came through the curtain together about 3 p.m. From his blue-jeans and M.I.T. sweatshirt I knew the surgical fellow had been called from home to work on me.

"I'll phone Coleman and tell him we're taking Robin to O.R," he told Lucy. "It will be a long incision. We have to check the length of the intestine."

I heard his footsteps fade. Lucy pushed back the hair from my forehead and said, "I called your mother."

The surgeon returned. "Coleman says we have to wait. I'm sorry." I knew 'I'm sorry' meant no painkillers while they watched my symptoms overnight. I was back in the abattoir again.

"Nothing more I can do here. I've got your keys. I'll bring your things tomorrow. I promised to tell your mother what's happening. After supper, I suppose, is best. Anything you want me to say?" Lucy said.

"I'm sorry I keep doing this."

"Don't be sorry. I just hate to see you like this." Lucy hesitated. "I love you, you know."

She stroked my hair again, said "Good Luck," and went home to her family.

A porter wheeled me to the ward. I had been in every ward on the ninth floor. This one, many times. The other beds seemed occupied but I didn't see my roommates.

The male nurse I called Mildred, pulled the worn and stained curtain around my bed.

"You look at the end of your tether." Mildred said as he put a urinary catheter into me.

"Almost," I squeaked.

My allotment of tubes complete, Mildred left me alone. Saline dripped then flowed through an I.V. into my hand. Vile-looking fluid trickled out of my stomach through my nose, siphoned by the clear plastic NG tube. A bag at the end of my bed drained my bladder though a catheter. Down into my intestine, through my ileostomy, plunged a red-rubber hose.

I lay spread-eagled, staring at the ceiling. My skin prickled with fever and rising sweat. I kicked against the covers to escape from heat. A corner freed, I exposed my right foot. I focused my feeling down to it, to the end of my body. In slow circles I turned my foot and spread my toes making them cut the soothing cool air.

My ankle made a cracking sound. My feet are always cold. My ankle always clicks. Nothing has changed, I tried to convince myself.

I heard dull footsteps outside the curtain and hoped they were not for me. I heard the curtain pull around the next bed and recognized a doctor's pre-surgical visit before the green surgical uniform showed beneath the curtain.

A light switched on, making the curtain translucent. Stains and patches gave way to enlarged, sharp-edged silhouettes. The curtain was a sham. It restricted neither sound nor vision, held back no smells. Neither modesty, nor privacy exist in abattoirs.

The doctor's silhouette bent and tapped on the huge rise of the elderly woman's stomach. It rose like a drumlin in northern Ontario, a slow rolling curve.

"You like to eat, eh?" came the doctor's voice.

"Il cibo è così cattivo." She sounded like my ex-mother-in-law.

"I'm sorry, Mrs. Agnelli. I don't understand."

"The food here is not so good."

Wonder if she came from the same part of Italy as Lena? Maybe she immigrated to Kirkland Lake too? Maybe she even knew Lena in Kirkland Lake?

"Are you in any pain?" the doctor asked.

"Just hungry. No pain. Why can't I eat?"

"No food and no drink for the rest of the night. You're going to have surgery tomorrow. Do you understand me? Surgery?"

"Yes. Surgery tomorrow. But why no food?"

"Did you drink a lot of bad-tasting fluid earlier?"

"Yeah, it was awful. Terrible. Why no food?"

"That was to clean you out," said the doctor. "You are going to have surgery here." His shadow pointed down at the ample belly.

"Someone will come later and put an X here."

The words froze in the air above my face.

A specialist nurse, an E.T. they're called, came the night before my first surgery, and with a straight-pin scratched an X into my abdominal flesh to mark the site for the ostomy, engraving the X so the site will be visible to the surgeons under the bubble-gum-pink coat of antiseptic paint.

Although I couldn't make out all her words, it seemed clear from her tone that the patient on the other side of the curtain didn't know what was going to happen to her. But I knew. Buried treasure lay beneath the X. Soon she would not have a bowel.

Tears streamed down my cheeks from the pressure and pain in my eyes and belly. The tube lurched in my throat and I threw up. I fumbled and retrieved the nurses' station call-bell.

"Sick." I said to the intercom.

I lay gasping for air, covered in my stomach's slime, as the young gold-chained doctor parted the curtain. His name came to me. Inch Worm. I sang to myself,

Inch Worm, Inch Worm
Measuring the marigolds.
You and your arithmetic will probably go far.

"This isn't supposed to happen," he said.

"No kidding."

Inch Worm kicked the jar.

Brilliant. He glared at me as though he'd heard my thought. Inch Worm tossed the curtain behind him as he left.

In an instant he returned, a kidney basin and an oversized plastic syringe in hand. Inch Worm disconnected the tube and inserted the end of the water-filled syringe. Depressing the plunger he said, "Do you feel that?"

"Yes." I belched as the cold fluid swept my stomach.

He retracted the plunger and drew the water — now tinted lime green — back up the tube.

"There," he said. "It works. Just needed to be irrigated."

I began to retch. "Leave me alone," I said between strangled coughs, and he disappeared again.

Minutes later Mildred arrived to clean me up.

"This shouldn't happen." Mildred counted the incremental marks on the clear plastic. "In too far," he concluded.

I let him remove the thick plastic tape from my blood crusted nose as I unfastened the safety pin on my soiled gown. Mildred pulled the tube slightly, slowly out of my nose. My hands twisted the white moist sheets. I fought not to whack his grasp away. Green boggy fluid rushed down the tube. I felt my stomach deflate as the current surged.

"Thank you," I said quietly.

Mildred met my eyes directly and said. "Shall we clean you up?"

He brought a warm moist cloth to wipe the blood from my face and a clean, but crumpled blue gown. As he fastened the ties around my neck he said, "Your back is red."

I grunted. Mildred massaged it briefly, but the intercom called "Nurse to 409," and he was gone.

I lay still, cursed my pain and visualized the full bottle of painkillers on the night-table beside my bed at home. Why do I let this go on? Why didn't I take them all at once instead of calling Lucy? The old woman on the other side of the curtain sang to herself, trembling over the notes too high for her dry voice. Because someone innocent would have to find me.

Tears dribbled from my eyes all night, though the waves of pain came at less frequent intervals. I lay rigid on my back, aching, one foot bared to the air, counting the blurry dots on the ceiling tiles. The night stretched long without sleep or painkillers. Beams from night nurses' flashlights spun and jumped on the ceiling tiles when they checked I.V.'s. Curtains remained slightly parted so the nurses could see the drips in the half-light without nearing patients. Crepe-soled oxfords squeaked on the hard bare floors as they responded to the call of the intercom. The rhythmic snore of the large woman in the next bed sounded blissful.

Muddled sounds drifted from across the room. I squinted my eyes against the din but saw little without my glasses. A rasp followed a long gust of air, like a machine exhaling. My right ear ached. A wave of pain gripped me again but passed away quickly. To my right the great whale-of-a-woman sighed and turned on her side. Her snoring ended and the room became alive with the sound of technology. Whirl-hiss, rattle, hack, hiss.

A gasp, almost human. I studied the sound more closely, counting beats, searching out a rhythm. The hiss elongated, jarred by a sporadic metal rattle. A whirl spun then halted after three counts. A lone smothered rasp bobbed over the hiss as though echoing a ghost. Across from me I could see only a rumpled pile of discarded sheets.

Two white nurses' uniforms shone through the darkness and spoke loudly to the sheets.

"Dell, it's time to move."

A breathy moan rose from the bed. A glowing uniform went to the end of the bed and cranked it to a steep incline.

"On three Dell. One, two, three." Without effort a white uniform raised a silent body to sitting position. I heard switches snap.

"We'll be back in fifteen minutes," one nurse said as they left the ward.

A little bubble of sound wheezed uncertainly in the otherwise silent room. I caught an iridescent flash, like the flicker of an animal's eye reflecting a flashlight's ray in a dark woods. The creature in the bed across the ward snatched desperately at the air above her. A long silence followed.

I squirmed against my imagination. Headlights catch

the unexpected red burst of animal eyes. Raccoon. I see it flail, its legs kicking at the air, the blood from its head spreading in the dirt. I recoil and hate myself for not going back and killing it good and dead. Run over it again. But there would be blood on the car. Evidence. Hit it with a shovel and move the corpse to the ditch. Too personal. Too direct. So I drive on and hope it will be gone by morning.

A chill crawled up my back and I shrugged my shoulders to release it. I held my breath, waiting for the sound, I knew would be small. I closed my eyes and concentrated. Finally, sweetly, a rasp, as the little creature across from me drew a breath. I exhaled.

The two nurses returned quacking to each other about another patient in another room.

"All right, Dell," they yelled. "We'll put you back." One lowered the head of the bed. The other juggled hoses and switches and the mysterious hiss began again. I raised my arm. One came to me when she finished her manoeuvres.

"Not asleep yet?" I recognized the nurse, Chatty Cathy.

"What is that?" I wrestled from my throat.

"That's just Dell. She was in an accident three weeks ago. The noise is her oxygen. Not much hope for her, poor-old-thing." She arranged my sheets and covered my foot. "Anything I can get you?"

"Painkiller."

"I don't think they're on order, but I'll check and if not I'll put it on the problem list for the morning rounds. Okay?" She checked the I.V. rate against her watch. "You sure are getting a lot," and with that she left.

I kicked my foot out from beneath the cover.

I lay immobile in the jaundiced light, and stared, blankly at the ceiling tiles. Paintings on the ceiling would help. Photographs of clouds or blue idyllic waters — perhaps some erotica. Images of broad, strong male hands on my breasts and soft persuasive lips on my shoulders fill my mind. Sex. Penetration. Penetration? All these tubes penetrate me, isn't that enough? Possession and aggression, that's all sex is. Who needs it?

The woman on the other side of the curtain heaved a sigh and rolled onto her back. Her snores bellowed.

I continued my discussion with myself. I have been in the hospital in every possible romantic state: married, married and having an affair, divorced with a lover, having an affair with a married man, and now alone. What does it matter? I don't need them. I can do this by myself. I've done all this before and I can do it again. Lovers just get in the way. I raised my arm with the I.V. to rest on my forehead. I must not mistake need for love or I'll hurt other people with my greed.

I tried to roll to my side but got snared in the tubes. Aggression and possession. It's the same with medicine. Surgery is aggressive treatment. It's taken complete possession of my life. Perhaps I was supposed to die in that first surgery, and that's why there have been so many more. It's all been a mistake. Why should God do such a thing? I imagined a deep voice pronouncing, "God created humans because he loved stories." I snorted. There is no God, just occasional grace when purposes collide and people rise above themselves. I peered across at the old woman connected to the hissing oxygen.

I lowered my hand from my brow and saw blood inching up the I.V. line. I rang the call bell for the nurse.

"Yes, Robin." A nurse I didn't know stepped toward my bed with a flashlight.

"I.V. is backing up."

"How's the tube in your throat?" she said as she examined my hand.

"Hurts."

She considered the dry I.V. chamber. The dripping had stopped. I lowered my eyes and stroked my hand where the needle lay embedded in my skin. The nurse squeezed the chamber, sending a gush of saline like a tidal wave in my vein. I jolted.

"Sorry," she said. "You're getting so much fluid, I guess the sites aren't going to last very long." She patted the sheets around me. "See you later."

Morning came slowly. Sick yellow light washed to gold, but the warm rays didn't reach the old woman in the bed across from me. No movement stirred her covers. Nurses arrived for the day-shift in starched pink or white uniforms.

At 7 a.m. the residents made their rounds without the Inch Worm or the Prophet.

"There's still the possibility of surgery," the surgical fellow said. He was American with a Beacon Hill accent, and I liked to hear him talk. "A simple obstruction caused by food shouldn't take more than eight to twelve hours to clear. We think this problem is mechanical in nature. Your surgery was last Tuesday, right?" I nodded yes. "It's probably internal swelling or swelling at the stoma site. We're going to leave everything as it is and watch you for a few days. Dr.Coleman knows you're here. We really don't want to open you again. Okay?"

"Painkillers?" I asked, squinting at the bow-tie he always wore when making rounds.

"Sorry. You know how it goes. We have to see the symptoms without interference. If your intestine perforates the pain will alert us first. Sorry." The surgical fellow screwed up the corner of his mouth and shrugged.

They moved to the Whale in the next bed.

"Surgery today."

"Oh." A pause. "Yeah."

"Someone will be in a little later to start your I.V."

The white-coated doctors crossed the ward and surrounded the bed. They clucked, bobbed and shook their heads in response to each other. One cranked the head of the bed up and another pecked at the sheets. Dell lay there passive and broken.

"We're going to take you off the oxygen more often," they called to her. Dell made no response. One doctor craned forward, repeating the information more loudly, but the surgical fellow caught him by the arm. "Let her be."

The doctors took formation and left, the surgical fellow leading the way.

A short thin Asian woman I knew well, nursed our ward that day. Her chopped black hair sprouted in no particular style. The green functional uniform she wore looked home-sewn. A stethoscope always hung about her neck. A tiny loop of white beads with black letters — the kind used on new-borns' wrists — spelled out her name. It was the only ornamentation she ever wore. She seemed completely devoted to nursing and she spoke often about the Homeopathic medicine seminars, Nurses for Democracy in Health Care conferences, and the Nurses' Association meetings she attended. She told me she had over twenty years experience. I never heard her speak of any other life. I christened her Florence

Nightingale. She ran from ward to ward, from patient to patient, giving lessons and thermometers, bed pans and weather reports.

"Robin, you're back. Couldn't stand to be without me eh?"

She made a flurry of activity around my bed. "All this fluid where does it come from?" Flo emptied and measured the output from my urinary bag.

"The body is fascinating, isn't it? Look at all this. Where does it come from?" She emptied and measured the contents of the jar connected to my NG tube.

"Anything else?" She lifted the covers in search of more drains. "Ileostomy?"

"Obstructed," I said.

Flo climbed the I.V. pole and reached for the bags of saline. Balanced on the wheels, looking at the curtain toward the next bed she sang out, "Mrs. Agnelli?"

No response. Flo flipped a half-full bag of saline over the rung and jumped to the floor.

"Good morning Mrs. Agnelli." Flo rounded the curtain but dashed back to me crying, "Where'd she go? She's not in her bed. The I.V. nurse is here at any minute. Where'd she go?" She bolted from the room, and it became quiet again.

I stared at the ceiling to avoid looking at Dell.

Not my problem, I said to myself.

I dozed between spasms of pain, their rhythm slowing. The blood technician nudged me awake.

Among patients the blood technicians are usually referred to as the Vampires, but this one had the big brown eyes and friendly gentle presence of a Golden Retriever. I'd let her do anything to me.

"Sorry," the Retriever said. "You know the routine." She tried to do her work on my arm but failed.

"Sorry," she said. "Make a fist for me. I'll take it from your hand."

I clenched and released a fist several times to pump up my veins then tightened my hand and looked away while she pressed at the tiny blue lines. I winced as she stuck me.

"Sorry," she said. "It works. I'm almost done." The Retriever collected her equipment quickly and said, "See you tomorrow, Robin."

I closed my eyes and tried not to feel anything. God I wish they'd give me some demerol. I don't want to be here. Demerol at least would give me some distance.

The bed seemed to sway and I began to ease into sleep, but the I.V. nurse arrived next. Unlike the Golden Retriever and Flo, the I.V. nurse remained an anonymous whitecoat.

"Where is she?" she said nodding at the curtain.

I shrugged.

"Oh, well. I'll do you first." The whitecoat examined my hand. "This has to come out." She ripped tape off my inflamed hand, thickened and puffed at the I.V. site where the needle had slipped out of the vein. Saline dripped directly into my tissue. She removed the needle and said, "Press here, please." I held a gauze pad against the tiny wound. The whitecoat slapped my arm repeatedly, turned it over and back. Bringing the goose-neck lamp down close to my skin, she hunted for another site. She rubbed a small vial of iodine on my skin and tightened a rubber band around my arm. I averted my eyes and counted the seconds against the familiar irritation. She completed her task and continued to the next bed.

"Still not here!"

She went to Dell, wordlessly lifted the lifeless hand, examined the I.V., lowered the hand, then sauntered to the window and stood, arms crossed over her chest, tapping her foot, gazing out.

"They can start the I.V. in O.R. I don't have time to wait," she said to no one in particular. She left.

Dell's oxygen continued to hiss.

Dull-witted and slow from pain, I know I must sleep while it's quiet. I try my tricks, counting ceiling tiles dots, deepening my breaths, singing in my head, but nothing works.

Flo zoomed into the ward. "Where is she? Where is she?" She flew back out, arms raised in the sour air.

The intercom droned: "Mrs. Agnelli, please return to your room."

Two black porters with plastic shower caps on their heads and red stripes on their white uniform legs rolled in the surgical lift. Flo chased after them, begged them to wait five minutes and whispered a muffled cuss. One porter laughed and the nurse hurried out.

The porter went to Dell. "How you doing honey?"

I envied his rich voice.

Dell didn't stir.

"You don't remember me?" Silence. "I brought you in." He stroked the headboard. "It's okay. You sleep."

He turned to the other porter. "My sister called from Jamaica. My mother's poorly." He moved away from Dell's bed. "She wants me to come home."

His friend shook his head slowly.

The porters left to chat in the hall. The surgical lift waited by the empty bed.

The inside of my eyelids felt rough as gravel. My

spine felt rigid. The tube in my nose stung. But exhaustion was stronger. Sensing sleep might finally come, I positioned the hand with the I.V. by my side, clearly visible to the nurses. The tubeless hand I raised to my head. The index finger vaulted my brow, my thumb pressed my temple. Curled around my nose, the three remaining fingers guarded the tube.

I was drifting when the bed jolted with a bang. The pink-uniformed cleaning-woman, I called Swab, stood at the end of my bed grinning a gap-toothed smile. She danced with her dust mop.

"How are you, my darling?"

She continued striking the bed-rails with her mop.

"Hurts," I said.

"Why are you back again?" The closer to me she mopped, the more questions she asked.

I pointed to the tube and croaked out, "Can't talk."

She began singing hymns and my jaw tightened. I waited for her to finish. It wouldn't be long.

"Gud Velsigne," she said. "You are a special person."

Swab always said that; as if pain guaranteed a place in heaven. I'd rather go to hell. I closed my eyes and sang to myself. The cleaning lady continued singing hymns.

Sleep was almost mine when the smell came. Grease. Nausea overtook me as the smell grew more distinct. Meat. I inhaled through my one clear nostril. Pickled cabbage. Opened my eyes and saw Mrs. Agnelli at the end of my bed, mouth open, a dripping sausage poised before it. I rubbed my eyes.

Flo charged in but halted. As the last of the stinking meal pushed into the Whale's contented face, Flo whirled around with a shriek. Mrs. Agnelli belched her satisfaction and climbed into bed.

Half an hour later the surgical fellow appeared in his O.R. greens. He drew the curtain around Mrs. Agnelli's bed.

"What have you done?" He tried to restrain his anger.

"I was hungry."

"You were scheduled for surgery."

"I changed my mind."

The surgical fellow paced between her bed and the curtain.

"You have a tumour on your intestine. You have cancer. Do you understand you are risking your life?"

"I was hungry."

The surgical fellow sighed. "Okay. But no more. Do you hear me? NO MORE!"

As he rounded my curtain he said, "How you doing Ms. Carr?" He didn't expect or receive a response.

Flo returned and collapsed in the chair beside my bed. She shook her head.

"Where did she get it?" I choked on the tube.

"Vendors out front on the street." Flo twirled a finger at the side of her head. I tried to smile. She brushed my foot as she left.

Lucy visited me in the evening. She brought me magazines, toiletries and night-gowns, my robe and slippers, but I only wanted my walkman, not sympathy or comradeship. I didn't want hand holding and best wishes, friends' good intentions and opinions on what should be done. After ten surgeries, what was there left to say?

Lucy bent over to kiss my cheek. I dodged, fearing knocking the NG tube. She withdrew, hurt in her eyes.

After five minutes silence Lucy went home. God damn me.

Tuesday passed much the same. The Whale's surgery was rescheduled for Wednesday morning. Tuesday night they started the I.V. Very early Wednesday morning a nurse gave her a sedating shot. About 8 a.m. a surgical lift carried her to the Operating Room. I tried not to think about scalpels cutting through layers of blubber.

Neither Dell nor I ate, so after the morning rounds, vital signs, and blood samples, the ward quieted. Oxygen hissed low and steady. I retreated into my walkman. Jane Siberry sang. I went to sleep.

A grasp on my ankle woke me.

"LaLa," I cried to Laura. Lucy stood with her arm around her daughter's shoulder. I saw Lucy's small muscular shapely body as if for the first time. Her dark hair, recently cut, showed more gray than usual. She looked stunning. Lucy smiled.

Laura had an equally sturdy build. At eight years old, she stood within four inches of her mother's height. I lifted my foot and Laura shook it, a gesture I reserved just for her. I had called her LaLa from the day she was born.

Laura put dark pink roses from their garden on my night table.

"Well, give her a kiss," Lucy said. Laura kept her eyes on her mother.

I wagged my hand. "Don't make her."

Lucy dropped into the chrome and plastic chair by my bed. She opened her red leather purse and pulled out a dollar coin. Raising it pinched between forefinger and thumb, she said, "Here, Laura. Go down to the lobby and get some juice. I'll be there in a minute."

"See you LaLa," I said. Laura peeked at me and hurried out.

I gazed into Lucy's dark eyes and shook my head from side to side.

"She knows what's going on. It's all right. She had a nightmare about you last night and asked to see you. We're playing hooky for the day together."

I don't want her to think of me as a sick person. I don't want her to picture me like this. The NG tube clogged my throat. I didn't have the energy to fight the words out. I closed my eyes and tears collected in the corners.

"Is there anything I can do before I go?"

I mimed a craning motion.

"Head up?" Lucy asked.

I nodded yes. She went to the foot of the bed and raised the head until I gestured her to halt. I was sitting up. I shifted, attempting to pry my back off the sweat-dampened sheets. The plastic mattress burned on my aching back. I found a cool bit of sheet. Lucy motioned good-bye.

Sitting, I saw Dell clearly. I closed my eyes.

The intercom demanded, "Keys to the Desk."

I caught the fragrance of LaLa's roses. I tried to turn my head to see them but, with the bed raised the tube caught me short, like a dog on a tightened lead. I inhaled again. Sweet perfume. I closed my eyes, dropped my head and tried to focus on the scent. When I opened my eyes I saw the NG tube filled with red. I rang for the nurse. Flo came. I pointed at the tube. She ran off and returned with a blood pressure gauge.

"You're stable," she said after taking the reading

three times at fifteen minute intervals. "I'll put a call in for a doctor."

Two hours later, it surprised me to see the Prophet. He pulled the curtain around my bed and sat next to me.

"I hear you've got problems, Robin," the Prophet said. His posture bowed with fatigue. I pointed down at the jar. Blood floated above stomach bile, not mixing with it.

"Is that all? Nothing to worry about. It's quite common. The tube is rubbing against the lining of your stomach and distressing it a little. It won't do you any great harm." The Prophet rose from the chair. "Nice flowers," he said as he walked away.

"Just a minute. I have a question," I said with difficulty.

The Prophet leaned on the veneer footboard of the bed.

"Will I ever be able to have children?"

"You're still having a period?" The Prophet pushed his lowered lip forward and lifted his eyebrows.

I nodded.

"That's a wonder." The Prophet tugged at his white lab coat. "If you can conceive, you can carry. But it's extremely unlikely you will conceive. It's not the ileostomy itself. You've had too many surgeries, too many taxes upon the body. It's unlikely."

The Prophet glanced down at my bared foot and pulled at the big toe. "I've got other patients to see Robin."

I nodded. He left the curtain drawn.

Usually, I leave the room when other patients are delivered from surgery. This time I could not. I gritted my teeth and put on my walkman, turned the volume up but heard the reverberations of the Whale swimming through a fluid daze of morphine. She rose to the surface, blew out air, took in air.

She heaved her great weight to one side and shrilly called out. She tossed herself to the other side and moaned. She shrieked. She cried. She groaned. I listened to every tape I had, twice.

Shut up you mammoth fool. What did you expect?

I ran my tapes a third and a fourth time: Miles Davis, k.d.lang, Jane Siberry, Mary Margaret O'Hara, Oliver Lake. My right ear pounded in pain. I drowsed between the Whale's episodes.

As soon as the Whale heard the doctors making their rounds the next morning, she bellowed.

"Calm down, Mrs. Agnelli," scolded the surgical fellow. "Rest. Rest."

"Why did you give me pain? I had no pain before. Why did you give me such pain!"

There it was: the guiding concept of surgery. Inflict suffering to avoid greater suffering. Did I believe in it? I suppose I did. Had I been born a generation earlier, intestinal disease would have killed me. It still could. I want to live. Does it matter that I can't have children? I can make things other than children. Stories, dresses or drawings, it doesn't matter. Nothing, not even sex, makes me more sure I am alive. I want to make things. I can handle this.

After Dell, the doctors came to me. My vision blurred from lack of sleep and nutrition, my head increasingly cloudy, I handed them a note instead of talking. The note listed my problems: the blood from my stomach, my aching ear and my declining tolerance. I used the word "please" five times.

"You hate that thing, don't you?" the surgical fellow said. He opened my chart and dragged a finger over a page. "Okay. I see the output through the NG was down overnight. I'll take it out for you as soon as I'm finished rounds."

"And the catheter?" I said.

"Okay. You won't need it after the NG is gone."

They left. I waited behind the curtain for an hour.

The surgical fellow returned with his hands encased in latex gloves.

"Ready?" he asked.

"Ready and waiting." I tore the plastic tape off my nose.

"Okay, sit up straight. Hold on to the bed-rails and say Yuck."

He took hold of the hard plastic tube and tugged, using a hand-over-hand sequence like a sailor pulling up anchor.

"YUCK!" I yelled and I meant it.

The tube dragged slowly as from a deep ocean to the end of my face, flipping upward as it left my body. A splatter of blood struck the ceiling, leaving a single round spot above the bed. I palmed my abdomen to check that its contents remained still in place.

Blood ran from my nose. The surgical fellow handed me a pad to hold against it.

"That will stop soon."

"Thank you. Thank you very much." I spoke without gagging.

I tried my voice again. "The Foley catheter?" My voice sat behind my nose and shivered. Half my words slid down my throat, the others fell from my mouth and tumbled to my lap.

"Pardon?" he said leaning toward me.

I pushed harder on my voice, making the sound go farther out from my face. "The Foley catheter, can it come out?" My voice was a pinched little cheep.

"Oh Yeah. A nurse can do that. If you start to vomit again, you'll tell someone, right?"

"Yes," I said reluctantly. I stroked my throat to soothe it.

"Sore?" The surgical fellow said dropping the tube into the waste basket beside my bed.

I nodded.

"I'll order some lozenges, but you won't be eating for a while yet."

I squeezed my breath to form words. "That's fine with me."

He heard the wheels on the laundry bin and exited through the curtains to see the nurse.

"Robin's catheter should come out," I heard him instruct her.

She called to me from the other side of the curtain:

"As soon as I've done Dell and Mrs. Agnelli's beds."

I sat motionless fastened to my bed by tubes, crushing my bloody nose with the pad. I listened without interest as the nurse shifted Dell and disconnected her oxygen. I stared at the trash bin. Even without my glasses, I could make out the I.V. packaging, flower wrappings, bloody gauze, the loops of stained NG tube, rubber gloves, iodine vials and white thermometer covers. I placed my glasses on my nose. My eyes strained but focused behind the lens. Blood stains turning brown at the edges of loosely woven cotton gauze. Scum coating the inside of the NG tube. I saw precise outlines, the shapes of ordeals passed. I took my glasses off and laid them within reach on the night table.

Crepe soles squeaked on the fake tile beyond the curtain.

"Need any help in here?"

"Yeah, help me with Dell. She's soiled her bed again."

I heard a moan and bedclothes rustle. The sour smell of shit mingled with the fragrance of roses. The mattress thudded as the nurses lifted, supported, tucked the sheet and let the mattress fall. Sheets snapped and were brushed taut and pleasant chatter rose from the nurses. They spoke of parents and friends, husbands and children, recipes for daily meals, voices cheerful and unguarded, the sound of women performing routine chores. I thought it must be a universal sound. It must come when washing on river rocks or working an assembly line. I wondered if I'd ever again have that ease in conversation.

The plastic wheels on the laundry bin rattled to the next bed. Mrs. Agnelli lowed: "The pain, the pain. Such pain," when the nurses made her rise from her bed.

"Your turn, Robin," the nurse said, entering my curtained enclosure. I recognized her. Erlinda had come from the Philippines. She had a three-year-old daughter. Her identification badge read Registered Nursing Assistant. Not qualified to perform medical tasks, the other nurses assigned her chores they considered menial. I called her Errand.

"What do you want first?" she said.

"I want out of here," I squeaked.

Errand smiled. "What can I do for you?"

"Catheter." I pointed down between my legs.

"Oh yeah, I forgot. I'll get someone."

I waited. She returned with a Registered Nurse. I spread my legs and the nurse removed the tube and left.

"My god, I'm free."

"More or less," Errand said. "I brought you some towels. You'll want to get cleaned up. I'll do your bed while you're in the washroom."

I swung my legs over the side of the bed and put my feet on the cold floor. She stooped and put my slippers on my feet. She positioned her hands under my elbows and I grasped her forearms. I felt her muscle bulge as she pulled me to my feet.

The room spun.

"Steady."

I waited for balance.

"I'm okay," I said. I used my I.V. pole as support. "Never thought I'd be glad to have one of these."

She handed me white towels which I folded over my arm like a maitred d'. The frayed edge towels felt coarse from heavy use and laundering.

"You might need these." Errand handed me my glasses.

Pushing the I.V. pole ahead of me with one hand and holding the back of my gown together with the other, I shuffled slowly toward the bathroom.

Has my body always been this long? It feels like a flag pole.

I opened the orange washroom door and rolled my pole in. The smell of antiseptic hit my nose while the jumble of bottles, stainless steel measuring cups, boxes of gloves, blue pads and wash basins confused my eyes. The door closed behind me.

I unfastened three ties down the back of my gown

then jostled it off my shoulders and down the I.V. line so the gown hung suspended in mid air. Bare, I faced the mirror. I leaned against the cold enamel and met my reflection. Immobility and the I.V. had puffed my face with fluid. From the irritation of the tape, a pimple blossomed on the tip of my nose. My usually pruned eyebrows had sprouted. Dried tears clung like crabgrass around my eyes. My mouth felt moss-lined. On top of my head, my hair matted into a thicket.

"Very attractive," I said.

I gazed down at the familiar scars on my abdomen. A bruise had spread on the hollow of my groin where the Inch Worm had taken a blood sample.

"Very sexy." I ran my hand up my belly. Have I lost weight? Yeah, five days without eating will do that sometimes.

My body started to weave. Wash while you can, I ordered myself. I turned the faucet. At first, I shivered as the hot soapy face cloth rubbed my skin. I caressed my face with suds, feeling the blood rise, my skin redden and the tears wash away. I filled the basin with water and plunged my head in, loosening my knotted hair to a soft fan. I swayed in the heat, working a bar of hand soap around my scalp, clouding the water. Under the tap's steady stream I rinsed my head, allowing drops to trickle down the length of my naked back and collect in a puddle on the floor. I lifted my arm, washed the black curls in my arm pit, and watched the mirror fog. A single drop followed the curve of my upturned breast.

I chanted to myself:

> *Thank god for soap and water*
> *for bread and butter*
> *for the touch of a sweet lover*

*Thank god for the ability to think
and the privilege of having feet.
Give me pause to consider lemons
and rejoice in tender buttons.*

With a brown surgical scrub I coaxed the suds into a lush froth on my pubic mound. The bathroom door swung open. Errand came in without a knock or a call.

"I thought you might want to change." She had a clean blue gown draped over her shoulder.

"Could I wear one of my own?" I kept my back to her.

"Sure." She went to fetch it. I patted my hair with a towel and pulled the dirty gown up the I.V. line to cover my ileostomy. Errand came back again without signalling. I started.

"Sorry. My little daughter does that to me all the time and I hate it. No privacy having a child. No privacy at all. She walks into the bathroom whenever she pleases. I'm sitting there and she doesn't care." Errand continued to chatter as she threaded my nightgown sleeve with the I.V. line. Finally, the printed flannel of my own gown covered me to the ankles.

I pushed the pole ahead of me and dropped the towels in the laundry bin I passed on my way to the window. I leaned my forehead on the pane of cool glass. An ambulance siren blared on Gerrard Street. I grew dizzy at the sight of Bay Street and beyond that, Yonge. I imagined walking, in my flannel nightie, down the congested sidewalk, pushing my I.V. pole ahead of me. Traffic. Noise. Crowds. The bustle of commerce. Well people going to work, and me doing nothing. The consistent beat of an air ambulance helicopter landing on the roof of Sick Kids mesmerized me. Organ transplants. Spare parts being delivered. I wobbled.

Don't push your luck girl, I imagined my father's voice.

I went to my freshly made bed and slept, dreams full of scattered images, disjointed sounds, broken repeatedly by the call of the intercom, the calls of the Whale and the call of my bladder.

Day passed into evening and the shift changed. Dell's daughter, a woman in her late forties, visited and cut her mother's nails. The Whale snored. I tried to watch tv but the food commercials nauseated me. Close-ups of steaming, bleeding meat rotated in space. Oozing pizzas were torn to bits. Hamburgers were devoured by fat-faced children.

They think this is going to get me to eat? I switched it off. I stared at my roses and listened to patients walking with their relatives in the hall.

Finally 9 p.m. came and the visitors left.

My heart dropped when I saw the nurse for the night: Gravity. Her breasts drooped. Her hair drooped. Her chin, eyes and uniform drooped. Gravity's many years' experience had only increased her indifference. She was slow to deliver painkillers, lazy in her attention to wounds and curt in her bedside manner. She came over to my bed.

"Back again, Miss Carr." Gravity slowed my I.V. so she wouldn't have to bother with it. "You seem all right to me."

"I'm okay," I said.

She crossed the ward to Dell. I turned the tv on and stretched my toes to distract myself. I kept one eye on Gravity as she fiddled with Dell's hoses. A tube corrugated like a hose of a vacuum cleaner pierced Dell's throat and entered her wind pipe. Gravity caught me watching and challenged me with a stare.

Just keep out of her way.

I lay on my side and flipped the channels until I found an animal show. I left the ear plug out and watched schools of saffron fish dance silently in cobalt water. Harlequin shrimp performed awkward pirouettes. Gardens of aquatic flowers swept the screen. The bed began to ebb and bob on the current when the glare of a commercial knocked me back to the dingy ward.

I raised my eyes as Gravity disconnected Dell's oxygen. Dell flailed and clawed, as always. Gravity stepped away from the bed and wagged her finger at Dell, until Dell's thrashing slowed to a twitch. Then Gravity took a roll of white cotton gauze from her uniform pocket and wrapped Dell's limp wrists, keeping a length at the end. She bound Dell's arms to the bed rail, then strolled out of the ward. Dell lifted her head and searched for the nurse. A few minutes later Dell began to squirm against her restraints.

Not my problem, I repeated mutely.

Then I heard faintly, "Help. Help me," in a rasp.

I rolled to my side, pressed my elbow into the mattress, pushed up, stood and wheeled my pole across the ward.

I saw Dell close up for the first time. Wizened gray skin hung from her face. No eyes were evident beneath her brow, only depressions in the bone. The curdling smell of dying cells surrounded her bed.

I'm here now. I can't very well leave. I untied the bandages. Dell's hands jerked up and dug at the valve in her throat. I caught her hands and held them.

"You mustn't touch," I said as gently as I could.

I examined at her slack, liver-spotted hands. They were tiny as a child's. Dell quivered. I leaned close to her as she began to speak. Her eyes, clouded to nearly opaque, faded back into their sockets, ringed by drab skin.

"What did I do wrong?" she wheezed at me.

"It's all right, Dell. I'm here. I won't let anything hurt you."

"Why are they punishing me?" She forced the sound out of her throat. She began to suffocate. I smoothed back her messy hair, dark at the ends, gray at the roots.

"Breathe, Dell. Please breathe."

Exerting tremendous effort she inhaled. I saw her rotting teeth were all capped in gold. Dell's whole body twitched as she exhaled.

"A lady came and tied me up," she hissed gaping at me.

"Breathe, Dell. It's okay. I'm staying here." I held her trembling fingers and stroked them with my thumb.

"It's okay," I lied as I sat in a chair beside her bed.

"Help me," she mouthed. No sound came out.

"Breathe," I whispered. "Don't talk. I'll stay here."

Dell closed her eyes and her body gave an involuntary shudder.

I noticed the tube implanted under her collar bone. TPN. Total Parenteral Nutrition. Dell didn't eat. A pump thrust calories into her body, bypassing her digestive tract. Five years earlier, I had lived that way, six weeks without food or water. I scanned the pole above the pump and saw dense white liquid in one sack and golden yellow liquid in the other. Milk and Honey, veterans called them. Patients whose entire intestine is cut out live the rest of their lives on Milk and Honey. Dell was barely alive. I was amazed to hear her draw another breath.

"Thank you," she wheezed.

"Shhh," I patted her sagging cheek. She's going.

I heard footsteps but didn't turn my head to acknowledge Gravity's presence. I let her come right up beside me before I spoke.

"She was frightened."

"I was only out of the room for a minute. I have other patients, you know. She has to learn to breathe for herself."

"She was frightened. She thought she was being punished," I slipped my finger under Dell's wrist to feel for a pulse.

Gravity laughed. "Punished?"

Dell opened her eyes and returned a faint squeeze to my hands. Reluctantly I let her go. "I'll just be over there," I said pointing to my bed.

Dell closed her eyes. Gravity inserted the oxygen hose into the socket in Dell's throat. I tried to sleep but the hiss haunted me all night.

Sleep in the arms of an angel, Dell, I thought.

Friday morning's rounds informed me I would start drinking fluids.

"Why don't we start her on Enable? She's awful skinny," suggested the Inch Worm.

I grimaced. Enable tastes like liquid chalk.

"You ever tried that stuff?" said the surgical fellow.

"No."

"Try it and you'll know why I don't prescribe it any more. It's not exactly encouraging to the appetite." The surgical fellow looked back to me. "If you drink enough, the I.V. can come out this evening."

All day I drank and voided, drank and voided, drank and voided. The day passed measured in fluid ounces. By evening I felt like a water filtration plant.

On the other side of the curtain, in the evening's gloom, the Whale roused herself. I saw her giant shadow climb over the bed-rail with astounding agility. A thump echoed as her feet hit the floor. I found the call bell and pushed the button. The Whale began to wander to the end of her bed, oblivious to her I.V. line.

"Yes. Can I help you?" came the voice on the intercom.

"Get someone in here NOW!" I yelled, my voice cracking from the strain.

The Whale swooned and the I.V. line pulled taut. Flo and another nurse ran in and found her clutching the bed-rails, her legs buckling under her great weight.

Flo coaxed her back into bed while the other nurse went to find Gravity. Gravity ambled in with a shot of morphine. The Whale squealed when the needle punctured her hip.

"If you want to get up, you call us," Flo said.

I drank more water and recorded the volume. Perhaps she'll be quiet now, I thought. But the morphine only aided her ability to scale the bed rails. She grappled out of her bed three more times and three more times was cajoled back into it.

I rang for the nurse a fourth time. No one came. I watched her disoriented movements cast in shadow on the curtain between us. Torn between loathing and pity, I didn't know what to do. I watched the pathetic shadow play as she lifted her night gown and wept over her cut belly.

She fingered her ostomy and said aloud, "Che cosa?" She began tearing the dressing off.

I called, "Stop it! Stop it!" but my voice couldn't cut through her despair.

I heard the plastic crumple as she fought with her ostomy. She wailed as she dragged out a staple. She looked under the bed and cried, "Vittò? Vittorio?" From the other side of the curtain I expected to hear a loud snap as her mind reached its limit.

Get up you coward. My will pressed me to act but all I could do was ring the nursing station again.

"We know. We can hear her from here. We're coming," said the box on the wall.

I gathered all my strength and lifted my un-cooperative body out of bed. I had begun to push toward the Whale when Gravity entered the room. I swerved, crossed to my locker and got my street clothes. I disconnected the I.V. valve, clamped off the flow of saline and pulled my body out of my night gown. I put on a T-shirt, jeans and running shoes before reconnecting the I.V. Pushing the pole ahead of me, I fled to the hall. I heard the weeping reach a crescendo from the corridor. Tears filled my eyes. I hadn't the strength to stand. I sank to the floor and rested my head on my knees.

I have got to get out of here.

I hauled my body up to its full length and walked. I passed the nursing station. On the counter lay the remains of a pizza and crumpled napkins. No one but Flo glanced up from the paper work.

"I have to tell you, Robin, it's raining and cold outside."

I hesitated then thought, the closet.

Flo met me at the door. I put my hand on the knob, but she stopped me from turning it.

"I'm not going back there," I said gesturing to the ward.

She nodded agreement and released my hand.

I opened the door and flicked on the lights. Crutches hung in clusters on the wall. I.V. poles made a forest in the corner. There was a wheelchair, a stretcher, boxes of medical supplies, and a brown leather divan. I lay down on it and relished its cool surface and isolation. The door banged and Flo entered with sheets over her arm. She made up the divan and adjusted my I.V.

"That should hold you till morning," she said. Flo turned off the light and shut the door. I put my head on the pillow and slept.

I awoke drenched with sweat.

"I've got to get out of here," I said to the crutches on the wall.

I rolled down the corridor pulling the I.V. pole behind me. I sneaked past the receptionist into the Prophet's private office. The surgical fellow sat across from the Prophet, in conference. I slammed the door.

Behind his teak desk, without looking at me, the Prophet raised his right hand to order silence. He then folded three fingers, extending the index for a moment's patience. The Prophet and the surgical fellow continued their conversation as if I were not there. Dazed and silent, I surveyed the room.

On the wall behind the Prophet posed photographs of his wife and two children smiled at me from behind the frame. A bottle of champagne looped in curled, multi-coloured ribbons stood on one corner of his desk.

Lining the bookshelves sat little mementoes of thanks from patients: two ceramic statues of frogs in surgical greens, a figure of wires roughly twisted held a scalpel, a tiny porcelain toilet bowl, and a kitty with bandaged paws. I'd been in this office many times; never had the gratitude of other patients so annoyed me.

The surgical fellow stood, glanced at me, excused himself and quietly closed the door as he left.

The Prophet motioned to the chair in front of his desk. I obeyed and sat, my weight forward on the edge of the teak and leather chair.

"What seems to be the problem?"

"I'm going to lose my mind if I stay in here any longer. I can't stand it. Do you know what's happening in my ward?" My voice was rising steadily to a scream.

The Prophet pushed back his chair from the desk to widen the space between us. Beneath his white, general-issue lab coat, his clothes were beautiful. The stitching on his gray swiss cotton shirt lay straight, even, perfect in its tension. His tie was woven in fine strands of blue and matte gold silk, the pattern an Art Nouveau replica. The trouser fabric, black Italian wool, was custom tailored to fit his slight body.

"You will lower your voice or you will leave this office."

"I tell you, I can't stand it!" I shrieked.

He stood and moved to the window, his back to me.

I noticed, as I always did when he stood, that I was taller. His right shoulder always raised with tension. I noted how elevated it was now.

"You WILL lower your voice," he said barely controlling his own.

I fell silent. I ground my teeth and waited for him to turn back to me and sit behind his desk.

"What seems to be the problem?" the Prophet said.

I didn't reply. We stared like two dogs confronting each other on a sidewalk, each waiting for the other to make the first move.

He extended his hand, palm down, so it lay closer to me on the desk.

"Listen, Robin. You're only in here for an obstruction. This is not life-threatening; minimal medical intervention. Relative to what has happened to you in the past, this is nothing. You weren't even on painkillers this time. How many surgeries have I done on you?"

"Ten."

"Ten. Many of those complicated, life threatening, and painful. As I recall once we almost lost you to septic shock and other times..."

"I don't care. I can't fucking stand it THIS time! I can't handle it any more! It's too much."

He straightened in his chair.

"You can't leave until you can prove that you can eat without your ileostomy blocking. Do you understand me? I will NOT discharge you until you eat." His voice stayed reined but louder.

I slumped in my chair. The Prophet rested his nimble hands on his burnished wood desk, a gold Cartier band circling each ring finger.

"Are you still seeing a psychiatrist?"

My jaw locked in anger. I will not be suckered into believing that there is no reason for my anger. I left the office without answering the Prophet.

I trudged to the chairs by the elevators and sat.

I watched the white-coated doctors, shower-capped

O.R. nurses in surgical greens, I.V. nurses with their tool kits, and lab-technicians pushing trolleys unload from the elevators.

I'm not wrong on this. Things have been worse for me, but I can't watch the Whale's or Dell's pain any more. Pain is too alive in here, too fresh, too concentrated. The next loud snap heard in the ward will be my mind reaching its limits, not the Whale's. I have to get out of here.

I shuffled my foot on the floor and considered my limited possibilities. I could take the I.V. out of my arm and walk out, or I could prove I can eat.

I stayed away from the ward, pacing the corridors and resting at windows. I went to the lobby and watched the revolving door. I sneaked into obstetrics to peek through the glass at the new-borns, but a nurse shooed me away before I could glimpse the new little bodies. I roamed the halls looking for a safe place. Eventually my I.V. ran dry, forcing me back to the ward.

"A post-ileostomy diet has been ordered for you," said Gravity as she hooked another sack of saline onto my pole.

"Goody g-g-goody," I said. My stutter had returned.

She snickered and left me to myself, the curtains drawn around me. I put on my headphones, listened to Miles Davis play and waited for the tray.

A young black woman in a pink uniform, rubber gloves and a shower cap put a plastic-covered tray on the trolley at the end of my bed. She looked shielded in her plastic. I wondered why food services people covered themselves more than nurses.

I picked up the paper menu. Pork Chops. I opened the lid. Before me lay two curled brown shingles with gray bones. Potatoes shaped to a sphere by an ice cream scoop squatted in one compartment. Over-cooked ochre-coloured squash filled a foil tart pan. The taste of metal rose on my tongue. Half a slice of white styrofoam bread occupied another compartment. In another, canned pears floated in thick colourless fluid. The design of the plastic tray ensured everything remained uniformly luke-warm.

From the napkin furled-utensils, I took a fork. With a single blow, I flattened the potato sphere.

You have to eat. My stomach turned. My mouth dried.

I dug the fork into the white mash. Separating a small portion, I tried to lift it to my mouth. My hand cramped suddenly and the fork clanged to the floor.

I have to get out of here. I know this game.

With my fingers I ripped the dry meat from the bone, wrapped it in the napkin and dropped it in the garbage can. I tore a page from a *Vogue* magazine on my bed. I wrapped the potatoes in a neat package and deposited it in the can.

Next I stuck my fingers into the squash. I lifted a small portion to my mouth and pushed it in.

Don't taste, don't smell, just swallow. What will this do to me? What is happening in my gut?

My fingers presented another lump of squash to my mouth. I ate it. Five more mouthfuls and I'd finished the squash.

To the right waited a covered cup. I opened it. Tea. Wrapping both hands around it, I lifted its warmth to my mouth and drank. Its fluid heat soothed my throat. I sat, absently rolling the cup between my hands.

Gravity came into the ward and lifted the cover of

my food tray. After examining the remains she said, "Very good."

I didn't respond.

She circled the room to check on Dell and the Whale.

Saturday morning the abattoir discharged me. Lucy drove me home and stayed only long enough to make sure I was comfortable. I was glad to be by myself.

The next week I vacuumed under my bed and in the corners. I reorganized the bedroom closet and the kitchen cupboards. I dusted. When I wasn't cleaning or asleep, I lay on the bottom of the bathtub, shower water bouncing off my belly, and tried to figure out what had happened to me.

Toronto Memorial Hospital

Patient Name:	Carr, Robin
Date of Birth:	14/02/58
Service:	Mark Coleman, MD
Procedure:	Revision of Ileostomy
Date of procedure:	10-04-91
Surgeon:	Dr. Mark Coleman/Dr. R. MacDonald
Assistant:	Dr. P. Ming

Clinical Note:

The patient is a known case of Crohn's disease for many years.
She had previously underwent pelvic pouch procedure but this
was unsuccessful. Eventually, she ended up with a terminal
ileostomy. Recently, her chief complaint was that the ileostomy
has become retracted and therefore now very difficult to
manage.

Operative Note:

The patient was given general anaesthesia and she was then
prepped and draped in a sterile manner. A peristomal incision
was made around the ileostomy and this was then deepened to
the subcutaneous tissue unto the fascia and then eventually into
the peritoneal cavity. By this means, we were able to mobilize
the ileostomy completely off the abdominal wall and we were
then able to gain about 6-7 inches in length of the ileum. After
the mobilization, we then performed another ileostomy in a
sprouting fashion. We sutured the ileum to the fascia and also
to the skin by means of 3-0 Vicryl. At the end of the
procedure, we were very satisfied with the ileostomy because it
gave a very good sprout.

P. Ming
for Dr. M. Coleman

CC Dr. P. Ming
    Dr. M. Coleman

The Leaving

Bells from St. Olave's church, beside the undertakers, clanged 10:30 a.m.

"Okay! Okay!" I heard through the ornamented metal heating grate in my bedroom. It was the old Polish man downstairs. Most of the noise in the house belonged to him. I wondered if he was shouting at his wife, Helen, or the church bells.

We lived — them downstairs together, me upstairs alone — behind a funeral home on Bloor Street West in a neighbourhood of East European immigrants. Ivan was almost eighty, Helen, his Canadian-born wife was seventy-six. I was thirty-two. Six months before my eleventh surgery I had moved from a one-room self-contained apartment in a generic low rise on Claxton Boulevard to the upper floor of their ordinary but amiable brick home. I had three small rooms, a kitchen and bathroom atop an open staircase and a shared entrance. Cheap, cheery, large for one person, close enough to the abattoir but far enough to appreciate its distance, this flat offered all I wanted. I didn't camp there waiting for something to happen. I lived there.

Tools littered our front veranda. Good simple machines, well worn from years of use, covered the floor and crowded the chairs. The varied tools of a professional carpenter sat, forgotten on the window sills. Ivan had worked with his hands his whole life, first as a carpenter-contractor, then as a metal worker for a refrigeration manufacturer.

I never saw Ivan do anything. I saw Helen on Bloor Street only on warm days. Always by herself, in a rose-coloured down-filled coat, a pink tam hiding her tangled long gray hair as she towed a loaded bundle buggy. She told me Ivan only got out of bed to watch afternoon soap operas, and she worried. The only way she could get him out of the house was to bribe him with pastry. They both grew plumper.

As winter wore on, I saw them together on Bloor Street. Ivan walked ten paces ahead of Helen. He wore a woollen black-and-red checked mackinaw, a brimmed felt hat and carried a long, cane-handled umbrella regardless of the weather. If he saw me, he just kept walking. Helen apologized after Ivan then struggled to reclaim her position two metres behind him. After three weeks he stopped to let Helen chat with me while he banged the umbrella tip on the pavement. Helen and I exchanged pleasantries: the weather, which bakery had the best sweets, the health of her three cats.

Spring renewed Ivan's vigour. After the thaw, the water-main in front of the house required repair. Huge backhoes and noisy jackhammers fought with the asphalt every day for two weeks. At seven every morning, as I closed my window against the racket, I saw Ivan on the sidewalk supervising. At 8:30, on my way out to work at Harbord Tailors, I caught him admiring the oversized tools, like a little boy.

After the disruptive machines left, in early summer, Ivan played with the awning's tilt above the front steps. I saw no improvement from the adjustment, but it didn't matter — Ivan was doing something. The porch smelt like sweat and effort. Ivan looked proud. And he made a lot of noise.

My doorbell needed repair, but Ivan worked around it. He re-cut inlaid pieces of wood he said the workmen had done too quickly. He pounded dents out of aluminium siding, planed millimetres off the door frame, and re-caulked previously well-sealed windows. Ivan tinkered with everything close to my doorbell but not the bell itself. My visitors would have to see him before they saw me. A short man with unkept snowy, shoulder-length hair, Ivan twinkled like Santa Claus when Lucy visited.

He worked on the veranda for months. He used a level to show me the precision of his angles. Ivan called me Squirrel, for my agile manoeuvring between his tools, around his shavings, under his ladder on my way out to work. Squirrel seemed an awkward endearment, one I wouldn't have accepted from anyone else, but it was still an endearment, a good sign for both of us, I figured.

Each evening when I returned from work Ivan greeted me, his paunch protruding from his stained beige shirt. He stroked his belly to clean his dirty hands. It left a delightful pattern. The soil-darkened sides of his paunch, like exaggerated shadows, made the clean section near the buttons appear larger, fuller by contrast.

"Come Squirrel, let me show you. Tomorrow I will..." he said every evening, and at length he explained the next day's plans. Each day his tools, glues, wood chips and home-made ladder barely altered position. Little changed visually, but Ivan seemed happy. Helen seemed happier, and it didn't bother me.

At the end of summer, as the air cooled and the light became more golden, I walked along Bloor Street from the Runnymede subway station, a pack-sack on my back. After years of abstinence, there was a man in my life. Men had occupied my bed but not my heart. I worried about the intricacies and insecurities of new love.

My lover and I had met on a train between Montreal and Toronto. Every summer I spent three weeks in the Eastern Townships of Quebec then took the train home to Toronto. In my mind I replayed our first meeting. As I scanned the packed railway car for a seat, I saw his curl-covered head bowed in concentration over a book. In a pink, three-button, long sleeve T-shirt, he appeared soft and self-contained. I reckoned he wouldn't want to talk and I could sleep away the five hour trip.

I settled back into my seat and closed my eyes. After ten minutes the train lunged forward.

"Ink-Alley-Jinx!" I heard from beside me. I opened my eyes and glanced at him.

"Sorry," he said.

"What did you say?"

"Ink-Alley-Jinx." He shrugged, "It's just something I say."

He introduced himself but didn't offer his hand, and I thought I had made a mistake. But time passed quickly. He told me stories.

"I live in Toronto. You?"

I nodded.

"I went to Sir George, then U of T, but I grew up in Montreal — Snowdon. My parents wanted me to date only Jewish girls so of course, in my adolescence, I thought French girls were real exotic: they wore make-up. I learned to turn sharp on my skates at Beaver Pond and spray them with snow. I could speak a little French, enough to order lunch, but that's about it. My father had a five-and-dime in Montreal East."

"My grandparents lived in Rosemont."

"What street?"

"I don't remember the name. Right by Canada Cement. It must have had a name. I remember we turned right after the flames and the towers."

"I'm almost embarrassed to tell you this. Working-class Anglo neighbourhood, my father the Jewish shop owner with French employees — women. And in the shop they all spoke English — of course. One Christmas I saw him and my mother hand out presents. He said a few words — only a few — in French. I worked in the store once in a while too. I wasn't allowed to date the girls from there either. My parents didn't think it looked good. I don't think he really treated his employees badly, but I doubt he treated them well either. But when he died, although the store had been closed for years, they all came to his funeral..."

When he told me he had avoided romantic relationships for the last eight years I named him Greenheart.

Neither of us could eat the processed food box lunch Via provided and we laughed over it together. A year of a friendship founded on conversations, on walks and over meals about books and movies, preceded romance. We knew each others' minds well before we knew the other's body. I told Greenheart that first meeting, about my illness but not about my ileostomy.

As I passed a bakery, smelling the lure of yeast and sugar, I heard a voice.

"Squirrel, Squirrel, come sit. Have coffee with us."

Ivan grinned from under his brim, behind the wire barrier that separated the cafe tables from the sidewalk. Helen clapped her hands twice. I smiled and dropped my backpack to an empty chair beside them.

"Can I get you anything else?" I asked. Ivan tapped his teaspoon against the metal pot, pursed his lips and shook his head from side to side. Crumbs dotted his shirted stomach. Helen had her mouth full.

"Okay. Back in a minute." I stood in line, ordered coffee and returned.

"Beautiful day, eh?" I said placing my white ceramic cup on the table. I pulled out the white plastic and aluminum tube chair and dropped into it.

"How are you?" I directed the question to the air between them.

Ivan's voice surprised me. "I'm going to Germany."

"Germany? What for?"

"Germany is united again. I have relatives."

"You speak German?"

On his fingers he counted: "Polish, Russian, Croatian, Macedonian, Italian, German."

"And English," I said sipping my coffee.

"And English." Ivan gave me a courtly bow with his head.

"I have nephew in Germany I have not seen since he was little boy." Ivan dropped his hand beside the table to illustrate a child's height.

"How long are you going for?"

"Five weeks," Helen answered without lifting her eyes off her strawberry-topped pastry.

"Are you going too Helen?"

"No." Ivan spoke and tapped his spoon on his white tea saucer.

"Why?"

"Someone has to take care of cats and the bird," Ivan said, his eyes now directed at the sidewalk.

"I can take care of the cats."

"NO." Ivan's voice was firm and quick, but he didn't look at me until he added: "Helen must do her work."

Okay, leave this one alone. I don't really like cats anyway; and that damned sick pigeon of theirs would make me crazy.

I sipped and watched the well-dressed crowd pushing imported baby carriages, walking pure-bred dogs, shopping.

I looked at Helen. She could have been my grandmother. She swept her long salt-and-pepper hair to a twisted knot on top of her head. Four barrettes secured the loose flow of hair at odd stops on her skull. Her glasses' frames, transparent pink with gold arms and temple brackets, slid down her nose. Her ears, not placed at the mid-point of her skull, but at the bottom third, supported her glasses too low. Her eyes floated up under the glass. Helen concentrated as she lifted her fork from the boat- shaped pastry. She wore a floral-print polyester blouse beneath two white machine-knit sweaters. A sheer pink scarf wrapped her neck.

"We'll have to go out for coffee together while Ivan is away."

She exposed her teeth to me. Ivan nodded his consent, though I hadn't asked for it.

"Ivan is going to Germany to have his teeth done. His nephew is a dentist." Helen sputtered between mouthfuls of crust, custard and fruit.

Ivan sucked his teeth and drummed his spoon more

loudly. Helen abruptly turned to a monologue of cat tales.

She told stories of her ten years dead cat, Tiger, pushing sheet music off her piano. "He didn't like 'Pack up your troubles in your old kit bag'," she said, as shine filled her eyes. "He always hid when I played it. It's the only one he pushed off the stand. I always thought of him more as a person than a cat. He had such a personality."

Ivan giggled but added nothing to the anecdote. He knew this story by heart. This was the third time I had heard it, but I listened absently, nodded and smiled at appropriate intervals. I fantasized while she reminisced. Every move my lover made enchanted me with its newness. My nipples hardened remembering his kiss and touch.

The tap of Ivan's umbrella on the sidewalk closed the conversation.

We walked along Bloor Street, Helen and I discussing the bundles of flowers and vegetables in green grocer's stalls. Ivan walked ahead but paused periodically to leer back at us. Helen walked closer to me and smiled without raising her eyes off the sidewalk.

That evening in my flat above Helen and Ivan, Greenheart and I made love a second time. We lay together, sharing the single pillow on my double bed, and whispering, trying out endearments. "Baby" he called me during intercourse. I giggled with delight. He mistook my laughter for derision and retreated to my given name. We exchanged secrets and strokes. We asked about middle names and family memories, details that were irrelevant when we were friends.

A few days after Ivan left for Germany I heard Helen downstairs.

She banged her door to the main entrance and shuffled her feet with deliberate loudness as she crossed the tiled foyer. I heard her check the front door's lock, mutter and bang her door again. An hour later she repeated the sequence. After I had heard her check the door a third time, I went down to see her.

"Oh hello, Robin. How are you? It's so quiet up there I didn't know if you had come in or not."

"Is there something wrong, Helen?" I said and nodded to the door.

"No, well you know Ivan left on Tuesday. It was such a time getting him off. I had to get his suit cleaned and his visa, and his ticket. He needed a new suitcase. I had one of those hard ones, you know the ones that have stiff sides, I'd had it since I worked at Confed. I bought it for a trip I took with my cousin when I was thirty. Anyway, Ivan doesn't like my case. And then there was the money. Oh by the way, when you make out next month's rent will you make it out just to me? When you make it out to both of us Ivan has to sign the back and of course he's not here." She barely gasped for breath between sentences. I inched my way up the stairs toward my flat, paused for a few seconds between each step as she continued talking.

"Sorry, Helen, I have to go." I said as I reached the top. She moved around to the bottom of the staircase and looked up at me, her mouth still moving. "I left something on the stove. I just wanted to come down and see that you were all right," I said, quickly turned the corner and walked up the last three steps to my rooms.

I went to the kitchen and put a pot of vegetable stew

on the cold stove. I left it on for an hour and hoped the smell travelled downstairs.

Three days later, when I came home from work Helen waited for me. As soon as my key fit the lock, Helen appeared in the hall.

"Hi, Helen." I looked over my shoulder to the cluttered veranda. "Can we put those tools away? The power tools make me nervous. Anyone can see them from the front step. Seems like an invitation to trouble to me."

"They make me nervous too, but Ivan wouldn't like me touching his things."

"But Helen, he won't be back for a month."

"Oh well, I don't know..." She dropped her gaze to the tiles.

"Why don't we just bring the power tools into the front hall? We'll leave everything else as it is. Okay?"

"Okay." She looked troubled.

I felt badly pushing my will on her. "You had your dinner yet, Helen? I'm going to go down to Bread and Roses for some soup, if you want to come."

Helen brightened. "Oh yes. It's just time too. I could use a sweet. Just let me get my coat. Oh the tools." She fumbled with her fingers around her hair, then around her mouth.

I still had my coat on and I was hungry, my usually small appetite grown. This is going to take forever, I thought.

"I'll bring them into the hall Helen. Where do you want them?"

She pointed to a spot on the floor between the heating grate and the door. She ambled through the door to get her coat. I heard the cats cry. She spoke to them. "Hush Beauty."

I moved a jig-saw, a circular-saw, an electric drill, and a belt-sander into the front hall.

"That Princess has gotten into my plants again, Suzy just won't leave Roxy be." She muttered to herself, closed the door tightly behind her and tied a wool scarf around her neck.

How did I get myself into this? "How is Roxy these days?" I asked as I guided her by the elbow toward the veranda door. I turned my keys in the two locks.

"Laying eggs. But it seems to make her ever so sick. She puts her head to one side like this." Helen cocked her head then shuffled backwards in three small circles, cooing on the leaf covered sidewalk. "Now you never see pigeons outside doing that, do you? I just don't know what to do with that Roxy."

I laughed and she with me. We walked slowly down Bloor Street, past the funeral home, the butchers and bakeries, past the flower shops and vegetable stalls.

"So what happens to Roxy's eggs?"

"I let her sit on them for a few days, then I take them away before they start to rot."

I gave her a questioning look.

"They're not fertilized, you see." Helen looked at me as though I were a child.

In silence we waited for the traffic light to change. I noticed how she hesitated at high curbs. I remembered myself, post-surgery, with a cane and touched her elbow lightly as she struggled with her feet.

"Do you have any kids Helen?"

"No, I didn't get married until I was thirty-nine. Ivan and I have been married for thirty-seven years. We met just over there." Helen pointed to the coloured-glass and cement facade of St. Pius X. "I taught English as a second language at night in that church hall. Ivan was one of my students. I can tell you Daddy was not very pleased when I told him I was getting married. My mother died when I was seventeen. Daddy and I learned how to take care of each other. We lived in a big house just over there." She pointed a pink gloved hand beyond the north side of Bloor Street. "The house isn't there any more. They tore it down to build the school. I've lived my whole life in this neighbourhood, you see. I bought the house we have now just after Ivan and I got married. I had been working for twenty years by the time I married. Daddy got really sick shortly after, so he lived upstairs."

"Where I live?"

"Yes, Ivan and I have never lived up there. Daddy died there and we had boarders after that."

I held the bakery door open for her. Helen chose the table. We ordered soup, bread, sweets and coffee, twice what I normally ate. Must be the cold weather coming on, I thought.

Helen told me after her mother died her father, a teacher, had sent her to the University of Toronto. He didn't know what else to do with her. Although she hated it, she completed two years as a math major. After her second year Helen took a summer job at an insurance company and stayed for forty-five years.

"I didn't know what to do with myself after Mommy died," Helen said in a tight strained voice. I reminded myself her mother had been dead almost sixty years, almost twice my lifetime. Helen would have been a young girl when women got the vote in Canada. Is the test of love longevity or impact? Perhaps Helen's mourning her mother is real love. Or perhaps that's just one kind. Do I miss Greenheart now?

Behind her pink glasses, Helen's eyes sparkled as a memory came to her. "It was so nice at Confed. They told me where to sit, what to do, when to do it. I even had an assigned spot in the cafeteria so I always knew where I was supposed to be. I loved working there. When Ivan came along I just kept working. I didn't retire until I was sixty-eight."

We sat together in the sweet-smelling bakery quietly drinking the end of our coffees.

"Heard from Ivan?" I broke the silence.

"Oh yes. He asked me to send him more money for his teeth."

"I thought his nephew was a dentist."

"There seems to have been some mistake. Ivan's nephew found him a dentist, but we have to pay for the work." Helen fiddled with her little leather change purse, her hands small, a little bent. On her left ring finger she wore a plain, narrow pink-gold band.

"Why didn't he have his teeth done here? Is dentistry so much better in Germany? "

"Poland."

"What do you mean Poland? I thought he was going to Germany."

"Ivan has gone to his sister's in Poland. He's having his teeth done there. He decided that he will stay away a little longer."

"When was the last time he saw his sister?"

"Twenty years ago."

"What's the longest period of time you and Ivan have been apart?"

"Six weeks." Helen sighed and suddenly looked older and tired.

"Let's go Helen."

As we walked home I noticed how cold it had become. Helen took three steps where another person used one. She walked, not lifting her feet, but dragging them forward, as if it frightened her not to have both feet touching the ground at all times.

That night I lay on my side, knees drawn up. Greenheart's head nestled into the curl of my belly as he slept. I stroked his abundant sandy gray curls with my fingers. I listened to him take a breath and push it back out. I wondered if I was in love. I wondered if Helen and Ivan were in love.

From memory I saw my mother bring my father a cup of coffee in bed. She did it every morning, even when we went camping. I grew up seeing love formalized in gestures of concern and comfort.

Greenheart sighed and turned his face toward me. He opened his hazel eyes and looked up at me.

"My mother used to do that," he murmured.

"What?"

"Stroke my hair like that."

"That's nice," I whispered.

"Yeah, well, it was a kind of barter. I picked her gray hairs, then she rubbed my head."

He kissed my lips. I stroked his hair and he moaned. He sucked at my breasts. They were tender and swollen but I wanted more. I kissed him.

A sound came from downstairs. I lifted my mouth from his and listened. I heard Helen drag her feet through the front hall. She opened the front door, paused as she went onto the veranda, then a click as she locked the outside door, a thud as she closed the inside door and a clunk as that locked. I lay back down beside Greenheart.

Helen and I had developed the routine of eating dinner together twice a week. Once in a while I took her to the Runnymede Theatre for a film. I had gathered the rest of the hand-tools — files, hammers, screwdrivers of every description — in a cardboard box, covered them with a tea-towel, but left them on the veranda. Greenheart and I slept together twice a week. Helen checked the door's lock every time he stayed with me.

"Robin. Robin. Good morning, Robin." I heard Helen from the bottom of the stairs as I lay warm in his arms, early one October morning.

"I better go see what she wants," I said to him reaching for my short black-and-red silk kimono. Nausea hit me. I redirected my grasp to a floor-length, green tartan robe, put it on and descended the stairs to Helen. She began talking before I was half-way down.

"I talked to Ivan last night." Her voice strained high and thin. She looked worn. On the fifth step, I stopped and leaned on the banister. I didn't want to get too close to her. The smell of sex was strong on me.

"I've already sent him more money, but he wants me to send even more. His teeth are costing a lot of money."

"Wasn't he supposed to be back two weeks ago, Helen?"

"Yes, but he says his teeth aren't finished yet. Now he tells me he has to stay into December." Helen fussed with her hair.

"Have you sent the money?" I rubbed sleep from the inner corner of my eye.

"I will today. So much for our retirement savings. I'll

have to cash some of our T bills." Helen shifted her weight from foot to foot.

I stared at her but didn't comment. "I've got to get ready for work, Helen," I said in a quiet voice. Why does she let him do this to her? Is that love?

"Okay. Will you be back for dinner?" Her hands now rested on her hips.

"I'll knock on your door at six. Okay?" I said and pulled my robe closer around me.

She nodded. I stroked my swampy stomach as I went back up the stairs to Greenheart.

We bathed, then drank coffee. I felt bigger, more porous, as if my molecules clustered less densely, sure he could blow his breath through me. This must be love.

In the kitchen I sat quietly holding the warm mug between my hands and watched Greenheart while I thought about Helen.

"He's not coming back," I said to the air.

"What baby?"

"I'm sorry, just thinking out loud. It's nothing."

That evening I started home early. In a Bloor Street drugstore I bought soap, men's shaving supplies, sanitary napkins and a pregnancy testing kit.

I took my sundries upstairs to my flat. In my bedroom I found Greenheart's black cotton sweater. I smelled his skin, sweat and soap. I put it on and felt his comfort all around me. I took my coat off the hall hook and went downstairs to knock on Helen's door. She already had her coat on, ready to go.

"I'd like to go to McDonald's, they have a Senior's special. I get a free pop, you know," she said when we got to the sidewalk.

"Whatever you want, Helen."

"I called the Consulate," She said as we walked Bloor Street.

I looked back at her but said nothing.

"Ivan's visa will expire in a week, and they couldn't tell me if he had applied from Poland to have it extended." Her eyes down, she scanned the sidewalk.

"Did you send him money?" I asked but I already knew the answer.

"Yes." Helen spotted a Christmas display in a shop window, stopped to study it, then said. "Perhaps we should get one of those bells for the front door." She pointed to an ornamented brass bell. "At school they used a bigger one of those. We could leave it by the front door."

"Okay," I said as I took her arm. "Do you still have friends in this neighbourhood Helen?"

"I suppose I do, but I never see them around anymore."

"Don't you see them at church?"

"Ivan doesn't like me to go to the English churches. Haven't been for years. We watch services on tv."

How much of love is compromise?

Under the bright lights and plastic of MacDonald's Helen recited cat stories while I ate two large orders of fries and she ate chicken sandwiches and drank coke. I tried to look intent but thought about pregnancy tests and sanitary napkins.

"You look really tired, Robin. Are you all right?"

"Yes, Helen. I'm okay, but I have some things to do this evening. I should head back."

We left. Helen chatted. I listened politely, without interest.

Upstairs from Helen, in my flat, I readied for bed,

though it was only 9 p.m. The rhythm of my life had changed. Greenheart and I talked and made love until one of us fell asleep. Mornings, at dawn or at my 7 a.m. alarm one of us woke and roused the other with a kiss or caress. By 9:30 we had left for work. Weekends moved like honeymoons. Evenings we cooked together, drank, smoked and talked while we cut vegetables. We slept together four nights a week, half of those at his place. I bought a second pillow for my bed.

Helen became annoyed. We ate together less frequently. I listened to her less attentively. My comings and goings shifted unpredictably. Two nights a week she was alone in the house. Now the noise in our house came from my flat. The sound of a large body moving, heavier on the floor than mine, louder closing the kitchen cupboards. And the laughter and noise of sex.

Mornings, Helen waited to hear him leave, then called to me from the bottom of the stairs.

That evening, about 9:30, I stood alone and naked before my bedroom mirror. I saw my face reflected hard, prematurely lined, anxious, and wondered if Greenheart saw me as I saw myself. I cupped my hand around my small breast and felt it bigger, heavier, fuller than usual. I wondered about Helen and sex. Did she like it? Did she ever have lovers? What did she think of me and my lover? What would she think if I was pregnant? Would Greenheart love me if I was pregnant? I went to the bathroom and weighed myself: five pounds heavier. With a fist I pounded lightly on my belly to the left of my ileostomy. "Come on start!" I said aloud and looked down at myself. In my head I heard the Prophet's words: Too many taxes on the body. I heard the Wizard: Bad taste in men. "Start damn it!" I said and pounded again.

I read instructions for the pregnancy test and went to bed.

Surely my period will start overnight, I told myself.

Early the next morning, before dawn, I collected a urine sample, measured a few drops of it with the kit's implements, mixed the powder with the urine and waited the specified five minutes. As directed, I poured the solution into the receptacle, added fluid from another vial and watched the dot turn pink. I was pregnant. I walked out of the bathroom and made a coffee. I drank it and studied the test again. No doubt about it, I thought, that dot is pink. I tossed the Early Warning Home Pregnancy Testing Kit into the trash can.

Pregnant. I counted on my calendar. How many weeks?

Maybe I made a mistake. I read the instructions again and did another test. It took five minutes. Another pink dot. I was pregnant.

I went to the phone, looked up the number then dialed.

"Doctors' Office," came a voice after the distant ringing.

"I am a patient of Doctor Greenberg. I've had a positive pregnancy test and I'd like to have Doctor Greenberg confirm it."

Then I left a message on Greenheart's answering machine. "There is something we have to talk about. I'm on my way to a doctor's appointment, but I'll call you from there when I'm finished."

I dressed and wandered from room to room in my flat. I thought I'd go crazy waiting and went out and did laundry. I didn't want Helen to hear me home alone. I didn't want to talk.

The doctors' waiting room serviced six family practices. Women my age and younger cradled and cooed at infants; children chased noisily around four rows of chairs. Elderly couples observed. I winced. A pain I realized I'd had and ignored for some weeks cramped the left side of my abdomen. I wondered if disease was flaring in my intestine.

After an hour's wait a clerk showed me to an examining room.

"You know it's extremely unlikely," the white-coated general practitioner said as I undressed.

"I'm sure," I said flatly.

"How are your breasts?"

"Swollen. I'm eating like a horse. And I'm tired and nauseated all the time."

The doctor watched as I rubbed my lower left abdomen."You know with your surgical history the chances are very high that it's an ectopic pregnancy."

"What's that?"

"The embryo is in your fallopian tube not your uterus. It's very dangerous. I think a standard blood test will take too long and an internal won't tell us enough. I'm going to send you for an internal ultrasound. The results will be definitive. If it's ectopic I'll admit you to hospital this afternoon."

Doctor Greenberg turned his back to me and phoned while I dressed.

I heard him say: "She'll be there in half an hour."

He handed me a slip of paper with the address scribbled on it. "My pager number is at the bottom. Have them call me with the results."

Before I left the building I called Greenheart on the pay phone.

"Yes," he answered.

"It's me." I took a deep breath. "I'm pregnant."

"Fuck. I thought so. Your tone on your message this morning was pretty clear. Where are you?"

"I have to have more tests. It's a high-risk pregnancy." I paused and ran my fingers over the cold steel casing on the receiver's chord. "Where's the glow? I'm supposed to get a glow." He laughed. "I just feel sick," I said.

"I'm here Robin. I'm not leaving town. Do you want me to meet you?"

"No. I've got to be there immediately. I'll call you when I know."

In the ultrasound lab waiting room sat three big-bellied women. They grinned, giggled, drank water. In their pink and paisley printed dresses they looked like chubby little girls. I cringed. Why should they be so fucking happy? How can they be so sure of life? I turned my gaze down. I never thought I'd live past thirty. I most likely carry an incurable hereditary disease. My body will make a poor host to a baby. That's a good enough reason.

The technician escorted me to a change room then to a dark room with two screens, a key pad and a high, hard examination table. A thin expanse of paper covered it.

"Had one of these before?"

"I've had lots of ultrasounds pre and postsurgery, but not an internal."

She snapped a clear cover, like a latex condom, over the end of a round-tipped probe. "This goes inside you, so we can look around." She pressed it against the mouth of my vagina and my muscles tightened.

"It will be much easier if you relax." The technician

pressed again. It hurt. She placed the tool in my hand. "Pretend it's a tampon. You can put it in yourself."

I concentrated, closed my eyes, took a breath and pushed. At the ring of muscle it resisted. I exhaled and pressed the probe inside me.

"That's far enough. Now look at the screen here."

The screen, much like a PC's, showed a little blob surrounded by a grainy gray mass. The technician pushed buttons and said, "You're definitely pregnant, and it's normal." Command keys clicked. "See that little part right there?" She touched the screen. "That's the heart. See it beating?" I kept quiet, my eyes locked on the grainy image. Her hand dropped from the screen. "How do you feel about this pregnancy?"

I didn't answer. The blob beat on the screen. The fan in the ultrasound hissed. Sam and I have a child whose heart beats, was all I could think.

The technician struck keys and a little cross appeared on the screen. "I'm measuring the fetus to determine how long you've been pregnant."

I watched the crosses define the perimeter of the image. The machine beeped as she saved the image.

"Six weeks," the technician said. "That's early you know. You must be pretty sensitive." I ignored her. More keys clicked then she said: "I'll call your doctor. You get dressed."

When I got to the waiting room the technician was already on the phone. She motioned to me, handed me the phone and said "It's Doctor Greenberg." She left.

"Robin. The pregnancy is normal. You're in no great danger. However, it's still very likely you will miscarry within the first trimester. Make an appointment to see me next month."

I didn't speak. I saw the pink dot, the heartbeat on the screen, mothers and babies in the waiting room and Greenheart's eyes. I saw a coffee cup in my mother's hand, steam rising from it, my brother's children playing on the grass in bathing suits. I remembered pain in my abdomen from past surgeries. I had felt the nausea, felt the fatigue for some weeks now. I imagined my lover's hand on the back of my neck as he drew me close for a kiss. I saw Helen standing amid her husband's tools on the veranda, her wedding ring circling a bent finger, shaking her head but afraid to do anything.

"Robin? Robin are you there? Did you hear me?"

"I don't want it. I don't want to go back to the hospital." I floundered among the whirling images in my head. "What do I do?"

"Call the Morgentaler Clinic. The number is in the book." He hung up.

Helen stood waiting for me when I came through the front door. The locks I left unturned so Greenheart could come in later. I had a bottle of scotch, still in its brown paper bag, tucked under my arm.

"I talked to Ivan this afternoon." She spoke louder than I had ever heard her.

I crossed in front of her and dropped onto the steps that lead upstairs.

"How is he?" I turned and pressed my back to the wall, then propped my boots up on the banister.

To concentrate, I studied her. As always Helen wore a plaid skirt, bias-cut so the lines fell in diagonals across her lower body. In summer she wore blouses, in winter different coloured turtlenecks over this same skirt. Today's sweater was coral.

"He says he feels very well so he's not taking his

pills." Helen leaned on the post at the end of the banister and stared down at me.

"What are the pills for Helen?"

"His heart."

My back stiffened against the wall. "You can't just stop taking heart pills. You have to cut down the dose over time, then stop. Call him back and tell him to start taking them. Call him back right now!" The selfish bastard's gone home to die. "Why are you letting him do this Helen?"

Helen smiled gently at me, but her voice turned caustic. "You know how men are. They get so damned determined." I had never heard her swear. "He's decided he feels good so he won't take his pills. There's nothing I can do about it, if that's what he wants."

"Helen," I said then hesitated. "Helen, most of the time I think men are just plain stupid."

Helen put her hand to mouth and stifled a giggle. Her pear-shaped body rotated like a child's inside a hula-hoop as her laughter moved down to her belly.

I put my head back and laughed too. Never before had I seen Helen sustain more than a twitter. Now she laughed deep and long. I realized I'd just said what she had always thought but dared not say.

Upstairs alone, I drank. My usual brand of scotch tasted awful that afternoon. I wanted time to pass. I ate, became nauseated, and tried to sleep. Lying on my bed, I remembered Greenheart. He told me just before he fell asleep he felt big and small at once. So big he could put his hand around the world. So small he would disappear in his sleep. I tried to feel small.

About six, I woke up feeling big, bloated. I went to the phone book and looked up the number for the Morgentaler Clinic. I dialed; it rang. A click followed as a tape recording began. A woman's voice gave instructions: "...location 85 Harbord in downtown Toronto; please use rear entrance; no need for parental or partner consent; if, however, you are under sixteen we urge you to tell at least one of your parents; please inform us of any medical problems which may affect the procedure; the fees according to weeks of pregnancy, in province, out of province; assurance of confidentiality; please bring urine sample; no food or drink after midnight if your appointment is in the morning; please arrive on time, with a friend; it is necessary that you call to confirm, the day before your appointment; abortions are done under a local anesthetic; the abortion procedure will last only five to ten minutes, but you will be at the clinic for approximately three hours; you will be able to leave on your own, but we strongly suggest you leave with a friend. Call the clinic's other number to make an appointment. Doctor Morgentaler would like to assure you that you will always be treated with the utmost consideration and respect during this difficult time in your life." The machine shut off. I hung up.

I took a swig of scotch from a Toronto Ladies Club glass I'd bought from the Salvation Army store.

I called the second number. I can always cancel it later, I told myself.

It rang. A woman answered.

"I'd like to make an appointment for an abortion." My voice's ease surprised me.

"How pregnant are you?"

"Six weeks. I had an internal ultrasound to confirm it, this afternoon." I fingered my glass.

"We don't do abortions until the eighth week."

"Why is that?"

"The cervix is softer at eight weeks so it's easier for you, and the fetus is very small, it's hard to be sure that the abortion is affective when there is so little tissue."

Such a little clump of cells having such a big effect on my body, my emotions. What will it do to Greenheart and me, my disease and me?

I said, "Well I'd like to make an appointment for the earliest possible date." I heard her flip pages in a book. "I should tell you I have some medical problems." The sound of pages turning stopped. "I've had eleven abdominal surgeries — I have an ileostomy as a result of Inflammatory Bowel Disease — It's likely I have a lot of adhesions. I'm allergic to morphine and all derivative painkillers. I'm also allergic to a lot of antibiotics."

"Just a minute please. I'll have to call up to one of the doctors." There was a beep, as she put me on hold.

I drummed my fingers on the blue plastic case of my phone. I looked at the metal grate over the heating duct and wondered if Helen could hear me.

Click. "Yes. I've checked. Everyone seems to think you should be scheduled to see Doctor Morgentaler himself. He has the most experience. How's November twenty-second at two?"

"Fine. Thank you."

"Okay. I've made a special note by your appointment. It should be fine," said the voice.

"Okay. Thank you. Bye." I hung up.

I poured another glass of scotch. In my landlord's armchair, I rocked, drank and waited for Greenheart. In high school, half a life-time ago, I had presumed I'd have three sons, Ryan, Jessie, Tait, in that order, as if having their names ready would make them appear. Children were essential to happiness in my parents' view. I had expected to reproduce. I had believed I controlled all aspects of my life. Prolonged illness taught me otherwise. Now I lived a full, happy life structured on the presumption that children were not a possibility. I had mated for other reasons. But I was pregnant.

Rocking slowly, I stared at the window and wondered about Helen. What had she expected? Had she decided not to have children or had it just happened that way? What did she want now?

From downstairs I heard a sound. Two doors opened and closed and locked. I had told Greenheart unlocked doors unnerved Helen. His tread thumped heavy and distinct on the wooden steps. I met him at the top of the staircase. Hands jammed into his short black cloth jacket, his face reddened from the sudden change in temperature.

"Congratulations. You're fertile," I said.

Greenheart smiled, mounted the last step and opened his arms. Although he is seven inches taller than me, I dropped my head to hug him. I condensed myself and tried to hide inside his embrace. He felt big. The cold evaporating from his jacket, he held me for a moment. He sniffed, put his hand on the back of my neck, then brushed the hair away from my ear and said, "You okay?"

"Six weeks, Baby. I'm six weeks pregnant."

He gripped me by the shoulders and moved me to the length of his arms. We stared at each other. My eyes roved over his face looking for a signal. His hands lowered to my hips and held me lightly as he performed a little dance.

"Hmm." He flung his arms open and mimed a dog's

pant. I scratched his belly and giggled. He laughed, "I'll have to start calling you Mama Bear."

I stopped scratching and moved away.

"I'm glad it's with you. My parents were nice people, they just weren't very good at parenting. They — my father really — were real good at passing along their fear. He came from Germany by himself after the war. He, not my mother, held the fear. She just watched him teach us his distrust. I don't want to do that." Greenheart unwound the yellow-and-black woven scarf from his neck. "I never wanted kids. How about you?"

"I thought the decision of children had been made for me, long ago. After all those surgeries I just crossed it off the list. What do I need kids for? What do kids need my disease for?"

He hung his coat on a hook and crouched to unlace his boots.

I leaned against the oak door frame.

"I guess it's a miracle," I said. He looked up at me. "I mean a supposedly sterile person getting pregnant. This may be my only chance to have a baby. It must be some sort of testimonial of the strength of our love, don't you think?"

"Six weeks? How can it be six weeks? We were just starting out. The sex wasn't very good at the beginning."

I paused for a long moment to make Greenheart hear me, then lowered the tone of my voice. "Women get pregnant from rape. Good, has nothing to do with it."

He snickered his embarrassment. "Of course," he said gently.

Greenheart moved toward me, then slipped his arm around my waist and held me. "The proof of our love will be getting past this pregnancy." He kissed my forehead.

"I suppose." I looked up at him and thought, we'll get past this pregnancy then he'll leave. I stroked his arms, then stopped. "Are you going to leave me?"

"No. Why would you think that?" He furrowed his brow.

"I know the statistics. After abortions relationships usually fall apart." I dropped my hands from his forearms. "The woman grows to resent the man." I looked away from him to the grain of wood on the threshold.

"Sounds to me like you're leaving, not me."

I turned and gazed at him. "I don't think I resent you."

We went into my livingroom and sat on the chesterfield. I rested against the hard futon then shifted to sit cross-legged and watched his face while we talked. He sat with his long legs spread, his hands between them.

"Do you know what you're going to do?" He cleared his throat and tried not to sound nervous.

"I have an appointment in two weeks. November twenty-second. Will you come with me?" I hesitated. "If not I'll ask Lucy."

"Of course. Whatever you want." Greenheart studied the spots on the carpet.

"Hold on here." I waited for his eyes to look back to me. "You don't want this baby do you?"

"No. But I want to come with you."

"Okay." I smiled at him. Pregnancy is just splitting cells. Love has nothing to do with it.

We sat stiffly, neither of us knowing what to do next. I reached again for my scotch by the phone. He watched me take a gulp.

From the metal grate came the sound of a phone ringing, then Helen's voice.

"Can I take you out for dinner?" I said, seeing the strained lines on his face. "I don't want to stay in. We should celebrate."

He nodded and grinned. I went to the bedroom and put on his black cotton sweater, a black leather mini skirt and silver earrings.

On the stairs I said, "The possibility of miscarrying scares me. Do you think we could spend most nights together for a while. Here or your place. It doesn't matter where."

"I already thought of that," Greenheart said as I opened the veranda door for him. "What are we celebrating?"

"Choice," I said.

I heard Helen behind her door, "Why do you insist on being such a bad cat?" Hurriedly I turned the lock behind us.

The next two weeks I hid, sick, angry and superstitious. Pregnancy showed on my face, invaded my privacy. I never felt alone. I always felt and resented its demands. Lack of energy restricted my movements. I ate, controlled by an appetite not my own. Crowded by hormones, my moods swung wildly. I wanted my life back.

Greenheart made tea and toast every morning. He did dishes, cleaned and went out to his separate life every day. Every night he returned. My flat filled with flowers and I felt like a rich woman. Many mornings we stayed in bed, made love, deepened our friendship. Other mornings I awoke with a scream from nightmares of being held down, of drowning. Often I cried. He soothed and encouraged me. He rubbed my belly when I sickened, cradled me, teased, joked and laughed with me. I surged and plunged on huge waves of feeling trusting his love more than my own. I felt skinless, nerve endings exposed and raw. Foreign sensations pressed in my abdomen and I worried constantly about miscarriage and the recurrence of disease.

During those two weeks, I didn't answer when Helen called up to me. I ran the shower or flushed the toilet to let her know I was home but busy. I waited for the thud of her door before I tiptoed downstairs to fetch my mail.

November twenty-second we awoke together quiet, stiff, blinking at each other.

"I'm going to get up, have a shower and change my ileostomy."

I shimmied across the sheets closer to Greenheart. "Do you ever wonder about it?"

"It just seems like an elaborate bandage to me. You never seem ill." He turned on his side under the blankets, extended his arm and cupped his hand under my bare buttocks.

"I'm not sick now but it can happen any time. There's no pattern to it. It's hard to tell what triggers it." I pushed at the covers and exposed my bare foot. "I'd like you to know about me. No one but me and the surgeons have ever seen it, the stoma — that's the exposed part of intestine on my side that's covered by the bag."

Greenheart followed me to the bathroom. From the cabinet I took two cardboard boxes, one held twenty white opaque plastic pouches, the other, ten flanges. I ripped open the flange packaging.

"This outside edge is like paper tape. It attaches to my belly. See, this part is sticky." I traced a one-inch diameter circle from a template. "Over the years I've had five stomas and they've all been different sizes." I took scissors and cut along the traced pencil line through the sticky center of the flange then squeezed a line of paste from the tube, like oil paint around the circular opening. "Glue," I said, then glanced up at Greenheart. "This bother you?"

"Show me the rest." He stroked the back of my neck.

I sat down on the toilet and pulled off the used flange and bag, deposited them into a garbage bag, tied it closed and dropped it in the trash bin below the sink.

"How often do you have to do this?"

"Every four days or so. More in the summer. It's no big deal. It gets to be like cutting your fingernails after a while." I wiped around my stoma with a wet cloth. "So this is me." I pointed down at my exposed red moving stump of intestine. "Sort of looks like the end of a penis, doesn't it?" Greenheart bent over and studied my stoma's flux. A little drop of shit filled the opening. "I can't control it. No muscle to contract around it." I closed my fist tight to illustrate. "So I have to work fast or I'll make a mess." I placed the prepared new flange, the cut opening over the stoma, and pressed it to my skin. "See this centre sort of ring?" I held up the white plastic pouch, "It snaps to the ring on the flange like this." I sealed them together, closed the open end of the bag with a plastic clip and raised my hands in the air. "Ta da, magic."

Greenheart kissed me. "Thanks," he said.

"I just can't imagine having it away out here." I moved my hand as if stroking a belly swollen with nine months of pregnancy.

The rest of the morning moved in a slow blur, our showers long, our movements sluggish.

About twelve-thirty we dressed and walked Bloor street looking for a cab. We found Helen. She smiled, a McDonald's bag in her hand. In a quick shy glance she surveyed Greenheart's face, then looked at me. She must know we are on our way to the clinic. She must have heard me.

"Haven't seen you," Helen said. She crunched the paper bag in her pink glove.

"I've been ill. My boyfriend has been taking care of me." I looked up at him. He forced a brief smile and nod at Helen, then searched the traffic for a taxi's light.

"How are you Helen?" I said.

"Good. Good," She clutched the bag with both hands "He's coming back."

I looked at her, mutely.

"Friday. Ivan'll be back Friday. It's been so long. I'm so happy. I'll have him back."

"That's nice," I couldn't think of anything else to say. I looked back to Greenheart. He raised his arm, lifting his short black coat above his waist exposing his peach-coloured sweater.

"Sorry, Helen. We've got an appointment." Greenheart waited for me, the cab's door opened. Helen still talked from the sidewalk as I ducked in the cab. His arm enclosed me, but he didn't speak. I watched Bloor Street move beyond the cab's window and felt sick. Will there be demonstrators?

I looked at my watch. As we reached Ossington, I said, "Let's get out at Bathurst and walk down."

We walked, my arm in his, and killed time. On Harbord Street I slowed our pace, looked in shop windows, stalled. At Major Street we turned, found the alley and turned again. Near the end of the alley, closed off by a yellow brick church, we saw the sign, noticed the security cameras and approached the back door.

Inside, a man sat at a desk with a sub sandwich before him.

"Carr," I said, "For two o'clock."

He looked down a page, then pointed, "This way please."

Greenheart and I turned the corner and walked into a long white room, brown plush couches at one end, cubicles along one side.

"Take a seat at the end," the man said "Someone will call you."

A woman handed me a clipboard and a pen. "Fill this out please and I'll be right with you. There's an information sheet under the questionnaire."

We sank into the soft deep couches in the waiting room. He read the information sheet and rubbed his forehead. I filled in the form. Across a coffee table, two over-groomed women in their early thirties gossiped. They looked dressed for a sushi bar, not an abortion clinic. Beside us a heavy, sad-faced woman waited by herself. I concentrated on the questionnaire. I read the outline describing the procedure.

A voice called me to a cubicle. The paperwork completed, Greenheart and I moved up to the second-floor waiting room. A young black guy read a magazine in the corner, a woman in her early fifties knitted, and the sad-faced white woman from downstairs kept her eyes down.

My name was called again. I shuffled into an office, the walls covered in framed movie posters. A woman with short dark hair sat cross-legged in an easy chair, rocking.

"Hello, Robin. How are you?" She offered her hand to me. "I'm Cheri."

We touched hands and I dropped into a chair. "Things have been better," I said.

"Okay." She opened my chart. "What birth control have you been using?"

"Condoms. But both he and I had been told we were sterile, so we weren't religious about it. I'm considering a tubal ligation, but I've already had eleven pelvic surgeries. I have Crohn's disease. He's thinking of having a vasectomy instead."

"Are you two married?"

I nodded no.

"Live together?"

I shook my head again.

"Well that's interesting. Tubal ligation is not big surgery, relative to what you've had. But it means another general anesthetic, I'm sure you know the dangers. Vasectomies are nothing. Let him do it. The last thing you should do is have more surgery." She paused. "You know, neither Crohn's disease nor an ileostomy preclude you from having children. It can be done."

"But what if I pass on disease? What if I get sick while I'm carrying? What if I am constantly sick after it's born? What if the disease kills me? What if...?"

Cheri raised her hand. "I'm not questioning your decision, just passing information." She smiled at me. I shifted my weight against the chair.

"Nervous?" She handed me a tiny pill. "Put this under your tongue and let it dissolve. It will help with the wait. We're running a little behind. Henry has all the difficult cases this afternoon. You'll be okay."

I returned to waiting room and waited. I snuggled into Greenheart and dropped my eyes to the floor. The bend of his long legs pulled his jeans up, showing his candy-apple red socks. I lifted my eyes, looked at his peach-coloured sweater and felt envious. I didn't have that freedom. I had to keep tight control over my image. For me, everything had to match, more than match. Clothes had to be the right fabric, the perfect cut and weight. I giggled.

He squeezed my shoulder. "What is it?"

"Muscle relaxant." I leaned into him and whispered. "I love you."

He pressed my hand and went back to his book, something with a bloody picture on the front cover.

I dozed lightly. In my imagination I saw the romantic, tv commercial version of motherhood: a young healthy blonde mother with a curly-haired, perfect-bodied baby. My mother was never sick. Married at twenty in the early fifties, she bore and raised three children. Mom had spent her life taking care of others. When I was sixteen my mother told me she ran a daycare because she and my father couldn't have more children, and she loved children. Can't do it Mom. I'm sorry.

My breath deepened and I floated. I saw Helen on the Bloor Street sidewalk looking up at me. "I've got him back," she peeped at me.

"You're better off without him," I said through the pink fog.

My head dropped sending an abrupt pain to my neck. I opened my eyes and gazed around the chester-field-lined waiting room. No one looked like a hospital patient. Everyone wore street clothes. All the women seemed childbearing age, healthy-looking, not like Helen.

I felt ugly in my faded blue jeans and a dark sweater, clothes I had deliberately chosen. I craved invisibility in the abortion clinic. Instead of my contact lens, I wore glasses, so I could choose not to see.

The two women from downstairs sat across from me. I scrutinized them and wondered if they had dressed up against ugliness. The blonde, heavily made-up, leaned forward to take a magazine from the coffee table between us. Beneath the plunging neckline of her black cocktail dress, a black lace bra showed. I looked at her friend: short, neat mid-brown hair, big pearl-and-diamond earrings, wide black cropped pants, short stylish jacket over a white silk blouse. A wide sash cinched her waist. Her colour co-ordinated makeup was precisely applied. Arms folded, tucked up under her bosom, she tried to restrain a constant fidget.

The dressed-up girlfriends snickered and twittered to each other. I listened politely distant. We all knew why we were there.

Greenheart leaned over to me and whispered, "Which one is having the abortion?"

"Who the hell cares," I mumbled.

I turned my eyes back to the two women. The suited, short-haired one rummaged through her purse, found a bottle of nail lacquer and began primping. I snorted at the smell.

She shook the bright pink bottle, "I have a black-tie dinner tonight."

I nodded at her and closed my eyes and felt the drug. My mind drifted. Does she think this is going to be like getting an injection? What is it going to be like? I want to leave, I panicked. I want this over and done with.

I remembered a test a few days before my first surgery, six years earlier. Without a painkiller to ease me, the Prophet had pushed a long scope into my bleeding large intestine and forced air to expand it. I had smashed my fist to the wall from pain. Things could be worse.

We got caught. That's what happened. We got caught, that's all. The consequences are mine. He's being kind and I love him. I felt a sudden angry rush. But it will be my pain, not his. He won't understand because he won't feel it. I wish I'd come with Lucy instead.

A loud voice burst my self-absorption. A short luxuriously dressed, European-sounding woman of perhaps sixty years, barged into the room.

She bawled at a younger Filipino woman with her : "Here, sit right here."

Obediently the young thin black-haired woman sat. She looked uncomfortably prim in a black-and-white dress, stockings and high heels. I figured they were her best clothes.

The older woman opened a *Globe and Mail*. "The world is going to hell in a hand-basket," she howled. The Filipino woman smiled automatically. Her European companion, pounded on the front page photo of Boris Yeltsin and Hemlut Kohl in Bonn. The headline read: *G7 throws Soviets $7-Billion Lifeline, Deficit expected to hit $350 billion.* "Look, Look at this," she yelled. Dutifully the young woman looked.

All other conversation in the room halted. I peered at the dressed-up girlfriends. They returned my glance, shaking their heads.

I put my head on Greenheart's shoulder. Time stretched, each moment weighted with anticipation.

A pretty adolescent black woman stepped from the third floor with a tranquil smile on her face. A woman in her forties, with the same calm eyes, stood to greet her. They hugged for a long moment.

The previously book-engrossed man moved to the bottom of the staircase. Two more women descended. A name was called down from the third floor.

"Barb," repeated the young man by the stairs.

The sad-faced woman rose from her chair and mounted the stairs.

The nail-lacquered dressed-up woman stood and kissed the blonde in the cocktail dress.

"I didn't think it would take so long. Sorry to leave you here like this, but I gotta go." She looked at her gold watch, then pulled on a navy trench coat.

"It's okay," said the blonde, "I'll catch up with you later."

The girlfriend left. Another couple, with wedding rings arrived.

Another woman went upstairs.

I heard a voice from the third floor. Then "Robin," repeated in a male voice from the bottom of the stairs.

I stood and picked up my backpack, "I love you, Baby." He kissed me.

I found the bathroom, emptied my ileostomy and went up to the third floor. My feet moved heavy and slow on the stairs. At the top a young nurse with long blonde hair, dyed pink at the ends directed me to a small garret with lockers and a bed. She handed me a blue paper gown.

"Everything off from the waist down. Go up there

when you're ready." She pointed above three steps to an open room filled with padded reclining chairs and other blue-gowned women.

The paper gown on, my briefs off and embarrassed by my red tartan socks, I moved to the next room.

"Robin." A nurse in glasses, blue jeans and a sweat-shirt motioned to me.

I crossed the threshold to the procedure rooms. The house became suddenly medical, white and antiseptic. I swallowed hard. Nurses moved with efficient purpose and I saw Doctor Morgentaler's back in a white coat.

"This way please, Robin." The pink-haired nurse showed me into a room. "I'm going to do an ultrasound to make sure everything is as it should be." She squirted cold clear jelly on my belly and ran an instrument over it without commenting on my scars or ileostomy. "Okay. Now give me your finger please, I need a blood sample." She pricked the tip in my middle finger. "Have a seat again. It will be just a few minutes."

I went back to the easychairs. Several women drank juice, others teas and biscuits. A red headed nurse in a loose print shirt moved between them. "I'm Heather," she said to me. The dressed-up blonde, now in a blue paper gown sat down beside me.

"You done?" The blonde asked Barb.

"It's sorta like a pap smear, but take the injection when they offer it. It helps." Barb thought for a moment. "You know I hadn't slept with anyone for three years, then one night, one night and I end up here."

"Clare," a nurse called from the threshold. The blonde stood and went in.

"Robin." I rose and walked in. A dark-haired nurse waited at another door frame for me. "I'm Jackie," she said and touched my shoulder. "I'm going to stay with you through the procedure."

She pointed to an examination table with stirrups. I climbed on. Jackie covered my legs with a cloth and took the glasses from my eyes.

"I can give you an injection or gas. Do you have a preference?"

"I think I am probably allergic to the injection. I have an allergy to morphine."

"Okay, I'll give you the gas mask once we begin. It's nitrous oxide. Henry should be here in a moment. Do you have any questions?"

Doctor Morgentaler and a different nurse entered the room and closed the door. "You have Crohn's disease?"

I nodded yes.

He stroked my cheek. "It'll be all right."

Doctor Morgentaler moved to the end of the table. I raised my legs to the stirrups. Jackie handed me the mask and held my hand. "Take a couple of good long deep whiffs before they begin."

I sucked at the mask, and felt the cold metal of the speculum against the mouth of my vagina.

"You're very tight. Try to relax," came Morgentaler's voice from beyond my draped legs.

Jackie looked down at me, "Press your buttocks down on the table and breath deep. It will only take five minutes or so, just hang in."

My vagina's walls opened. I pushed down hard on the table and the mask. I sucked and tried not to squirm. I tried to separate my head from the sensation in my abdomen. I looked up at Jackie. She squeezed my hand. I shut my eyes.

"They swab your cervix with antiseptic now. Did you

217

feel that? Then they'll freeze it, like a dentist freezes your gums."

I flinched. I sucked at the gas, hoped for sleep, but felt the dilators. I heard a machine, and opened my eyes to find Jackie's reassurance.

"That's suction. You're doing fine." I heard Morgentaler say.

"Next there'll be some scraping, to make sure the placenta has been removed."

"Here come the cramps," I mumbled behind the mask as spasms of pain flowed from my abdomen to my head. My ileostomy gurgled. I squeezed my eyes shut and tried not to record any sounds, any sensations.

I heard the suction begin again. "We're almost done."

It was over.

Morgentaler moved to the head of my table. "Okay?"

I nodded yes. He stroked my cheek again before he left.

I lay still, wordless for a few moments and felt my breath and my belly contract in pain before I walked into the recovery room.

Heather guided me to an easychair and covered me with a blanket.

Clare smiled at me. I closed my eyes. Heather brought me some apple juice. I sipped it. I doubled over and vomited. I heard Heather's voice and felt her hand on the back of my head. She lowered my socks from my knees to my ankles and opened the back of my paper gown.

"Stay down," she said to me. "Cover up," she said to everyone else.

My sight went blank. My head buzzed. The room whirled.

"When you feel cold you'll be okay." I heard a door open.

Sweat ran down my back and my knees. I hacked and gagged. A warm hand spread on my back, then two hands on my knees.

I sat up and saw Heather. "Easy," she said, "Easy. Deep breaths. Sit back."

Jackie handed me a cup. "Tylenol 3s." I took two white pills and washed them down with apple juice. Heather put her hands under my armpits, lifted and led me to the bed in the garret. "Lay here for a while. You'll be okay. It's just harder on some people than others. Take it easy for a little while. But come and see me before you leave."

I lay in the bed. I think I slept. Other women came into the room and put on blue paper gowns. Clare came in, slipped into her black cocktail dress, sheer stockings and heels. I heard her voice mingle with Heather's. Clare's heels clicked on the stairs to the second floor.

I rose from the bed, put on my jeans and sweater and wandered in a fog back to the recovery room.

Heather took hold of my elbow and handed me a brown paper envelope. "There's a follow-up information sheet in here." She opened the envelope and withdrew two tiny packets. "Antibiotics. Take all of them. These other pills firm up your uterus. They should be taken immediately, but if you're just going to throw them up you can wait until tomorrow. These," Heather held out string of six packaged condoms, "I presume you know what to do with, but no intercourse for two weeks. You can leave if you want, but I think it's a bit early. You still look green around the gills."

I turned and wobbled down the stairs. I saw Greenheart pacing in the waiting room. He came to me and I collapsed in his arms.

"Get me out of here," I moaned.

He helped me with my coat and directed me to the first floor.

"Did you call for a taxi?" A woman's voice spoke to Greenheart.

"No, I think that was Clare," I answered.

The woman shrugged and moved toward the front door. "I just saw Clare leave."

"We'll take it." Greenheart said, his hand still under my elbow. I leaned into him.

We left, by the front door of the Morgentaler Clinic, into Friday rush-hour on Harbord Street.

Facts about Inflammatory Bowel Disease
from the Crohn's and Colitis Foundation of Canada

- IBD can and does strike anyone regardless of age, sex or race. It is a chronic and non-contagious disease with no known cause or cure.

- IBD is not an emotional disorder. Crohn's and Ulcerative Colitis are not caused by stress or anxiety nor restricted to certain personality types.

- Crohn's and Ulcerative Colitis strike most frequently between the ages of 15 and 35. About 20% of sufferers are children.

- Although some drug treatment is available to IBD patients, Crohn's Disease remains incurable. Sometimes radical surgery helps, sometimes it doesn't.

- Approximately 18% of patients with IBD have family members with either Ulcerative Colitis or Crohn's. This familial aggregation of IBD is probably genetic rather than the result of a common environmental factor; however to date no genetic markers have been found to support a genetic basis for IBD.

- Both disorders occur worldwide. The diseases occur most frequently in northern Europe and North America, with less frequency in Central Europe, the Middle east and Australia, and least frequently in Asia and Africa. The annual incidence of IBD worldwide is from 5 to 15 new cases per 100,000 population in countries where it has been studied.

- The incidence of inflammatory bowel disease in Canada is among the highest in the world. An often quoted statistic is 1 out of every 100 Canadians has IBD.

- Since its establishment in 1974, the Crohn's and Colitis Foundation of Canada has been committed to the funding of medical research into the cause and cure of Inflammatory Bowel Disease. The Foundation directs 75% of the total funds raised each year to research and education. The Foundation has awarded over $14 million to more than 100 research projects and to the establishment of two intestinal disease research units in Calgary, Alberta and Hamilton, Ontario.

DONNA McFARLANE was born in Montreal in 1958, grew up there and in Ottawa, and moved to Toronto in 1977 to attend York University. She first became ill with Inflammatory Bowel Disease in 1984. Since then she has endured many hospitalizations and twelve abdominal surgeries. Donna McFarlane recently co-wrote a collection of short stories called *Dishrag*.